Something Bright

A Being(s) in Love Story

R. Cooper

Copyright © 2022 R. Cooper

All rights reserved

ISBN 9798443172583

This is a work of fiction. Names, characters, businesses, places, events, locales, and incidents are either the products of the author's imagination or used in a fictitious manner. Any resemblance to actual persons, living or dead, or actual events is purely coincidental.

Cover art by Lyn Forester

Content tags: An old-fashioned view of addiction, sobriety, and recovery. Alcoholism, drinking, smoking. Guns are onpage but not used. Some gambling onpage. Mention of past sex work. Brief mention of part of some of California's more shameful history. Onpage sex. Late 19th century attitudes toward gender roles and femininity, and one character's navigation of those.

Contents

1.	One	1
2.	Two	19
3.	Three	43
4.	Epilogue	63
	The Being(s) in Love Series	81
	Also By R. Cooper	82
	About R. Cooper	83

One

BATCH got herself a room in a house owned by a sweet but prone-to-tippling older widow because nights got cold, especially down in the valley, and when Batch wasn't restlessly patrolling the streets and waiting for something to happen, she wanted to rest someplace to keep a body warm until she had to face the light of morning. She valued warmth, these days, in a way she hadn't when she'd been twenty and wilder. Or maybe warmth was just something she could give herself now that things were quiet and her mind was no longer focused on one thing only.

She could have stayed at the hotel, which mostly held people passing through this collection of streets on its way to being a town but had a few full-time boarders. Batch would have been welcome. Carillo lived there, after all, and so did the girl, his girl, who had been one of those passing through but had stayed for him, even if neither of them acknowledged that yet. But once Batch had truly been able to call herself sobered up and the time had come to stop bunking at the jail with Tinney, her feet had carried her in the opposite direction, away from the St. Christopher Hotel.

Not out of town. Not that far. Not back up into the hills to the logging camps, and not farther south to bigger places like Los Cerros. Just to the edge of the main streets and down a few alleys. Out of sight, with the wandering farmhands, and the miners who had never found their fortunes, and the girls who didn't work out of the house up the road toward the geysers and the health resort for the wealthy.

Her room had a chest of drawers she used as a wash stand also, and a tiny table with a lamp on it next to the bed. The mattress was small and full of lumps compared to the dozens of mattresses Batch had visited since she'd started life on her own, but she also compared it to stables and pigsties and just plain hard-packed dirt, and knew that small and lumpy wasn't so bad. And it wasn't as though there was a body next to her to share it and take up space. So the mattress was fine, more than fine; it was something to be grateful for.

The chest of drawers was mostly empty. Batch was earning pay now, steady pay, and would be at least for a while, but had only been doing so for a few months. She owned the clothes she had on, and some spare shirts and underthings, and a hairbrush and some pins. That was all she'd replaced once she had spending money. Everything else she'd once owned had been sold or stolen years ago.

In quiet moments, she thought maybe she was afraid to have things again. Not because she might be tempted to sell them for a drink, although she might, but because she couldn't be trusted with anything precious, not even a hand-mirror or a kerchief nicer than the one she wore around her neck on hotter days. That was just a scrap of red, one of Tinney's, given as a gift.

The old man was kind, in his way, though he tried his best to disguise it with constant grumbles and hushed insults for the people he didn't approve of. Batch wasn't one of them. She still didn't know why, but she was grateful for that as well.

Tinney had once had a small homestead and lost it, either through cards or a debt, Batch didn't know. But for all that he was rough, he'd been the sort to keep books in his house and still was, despite living at the jailhouse. He knew his prayers backwards and forwards but had used his rifle on a man or two, or threatened to and meant it, and he had Carillo's gruff admiration. With all of that, and being there to witness Batch sick all over herself and shaking and crying and whatever else she'd done in that first week of sobriety, he still thought she was worth conversation and a little gift.

Batch thought about that in quiet moments too. But she had a lot of quiet moments these days. The whole town did, now that the dust-ups were mostly whiskey-soaked loggers and gamblers and the like getting in trouble, and not disputes people had thought to settle with guns, and on one occasion, a hatchet, or farther inland, a shameful massacre, although most in town didn't speak of that.

The nights Batch wasn't working, she woke with her back to the wall; some nights shivering even with her blankets around her, and blinking up at her ceiling like a kid stared at the painted ceilings of the tall buildings in big cities.

It wasn't a tent and it wasn't the sky. It was a ceiling, and above that was a roof. She had a bed and a mostly empty chest of drawers. Not much else, but she had those. Pathetic, she supposed, to the landowners and the rich ladies heading up to the geysers for the hot springs and their health.

Batch had been all over, in her somewhere-near to twenty-six or twenty-seven years, but she'd had a place of her own only a handful of times, and never as a cleaned-up, genuine member of the world.

It was something else to think about.

Worry about.

Fret over while she pinned up her hair and got dressed to go walk through town in her vest and shirt and her long men's trousers. In the old days, when she'd been a kid with her pa newly buried, the area had been full of people on their way elsewhere, prospectors and speculators heading north to find money or heading south to spend it, poor miners on their way to misery up in the mountains, and a few Pomo heading away from those others. Batch wearing men's clothes had been just how it was, cheaper and easier and sort of a joke. Everyone then had been more concerned with themselves than anyone else. Nobody proper had been around to care what someone else was wearing unless it was worth something. So, except for a brief stint in one of the towns down near Los Cerros, Batch had never attempted women's weeds, and those had been borrowed flash.

But those days were gone. The valley, and the hills and mountains around it, was an area on the verge of settling down. The town would get a name soon, and probably officially elect Carillo as their sheriff, instead of just paying him to stop the bloodshed between drunken loggers and farmers and high-and-mighty landowners as needed.

It was possibly no place for Batch with her pants and her gun and her belt with the work knife tucked into it. It was definitely no place for Blue, even if she hadn't been Blue for half a year now.

Six months, even if no one had said a word about it to her face. Batch could still smell the piss and sweat on herself sometimes no matter how much she bathed, still lick the sick from her teeth and taste something sweet and burning hot on her breath, dry in the back of her throat. No one would say a word, not with Carillo and Tinney standing guard like a pair of tough, cranky hens, and not after seeing Batch's temper.

But no one really needed to; it hung in the air behind her like echo after rifle fire, the metallic burst ringing in her ears. Her name. Her old name, a nickname to replace the first, but Batch had been called Batch so long she'd forgotten to be bothered by it.

She washed her face and hands in the bowl on her dresser, and patted her face dry without letting her gaze catch in the dresser mirror. She was a blur, sundarkened face and brown hair twisted back and off her neck. Her shirt was the color of sand and her pants and vest only a little darker. She tied Tinney's scarf around her neck to see something bright, and only then looked up, just for a moment. Her cheekbones were prominent, making her feel as rawboned as ever. Her mouth was wide and her brows serious. But her eyes were clear.

She blew out a breath, then bent down to ensure her gun stayed strapped to her thigh.

Showy, having a pistol handy like that, as if she were a gunslinger from a dime novel. But it helped to have it out and noticeable, made people less inclined to challenge her. Carillo wore one in his belt, and sometimes kept a small pistol in his coat pocket, but he was more the kind to carry a heavy stick and speak in a voice that carried.

Foolish people had tried to cross him anyway. Frequently, when this town hadn't been more than a place for the stage drivers to get water and food and pick up mail, but most famously about six months ago. Which was why Batch had clear eyes and a shooter on her thigh. She fancied Carillo might end up a legend for that whole affair, or if not that, then for the fact that he had the same name as one of the wealthiest families around, but if he was asked about it, wouldn't say a word.

He was the legendary kind, despite his broken nose, and being half a head shorter than Batch, who wasn't overly tall, and how he always wore the same black shirt day in and day out.

Batch was more than a little surprised her nose had never been broken, although she'd had a tooth knocked out on one side of her mouth and had scars along her knuckles. She glanced at herself in the mirror one last time to make sure that if Tinney asked her if she was all right, she would look all right when she answered, then she turned the lamp down and off and left the room.

She didn't have oils or perfumes to put in her hair, but she bathed twice a week now that she had some coin in her pocket. It was about the only thing she'd ever dreamed of after a roof over her head, and she had nothing to save the money for anyway. Her landlady washed and ironed her clothes for her, and used lavender in her laundry soap. The fancy touch was a waste for someone like Batch, who was probably going to wind up walking another drunk down to the jail to sleep it off and smell like their whiskey and sick by morning.

Batch didn't ask her landlady to stop, though.

There was no sign of the old widow out in front of the boarding house when Batch came down the stairs and then around to the front of the building. Batch's room was in the back, overlooking a tiny yard between the house and what had briefly been the office of a dentist, with a shared outhouse.

Batch walked on, glancing first up to the sky, which would cover over in clouds through the night, which would then disappear by noon tomorrow. Satisfied it wasn't set to rain, she continued on, looking idly and then not idly around the street.

Things seemed busier than usual, a touch more crowded around the cantina at her end of town and also farther up the main street, by the hotel. Visitors in town, probably on a stage or a private carriage or two heading up to the geysers or beyond.

Batch slowed to barely more than a stroll while she considered grabbing a bite at the stand outside the cantina where they sold food for anyone not willing or not allowed to go inside to gamble or drink. She wasn't due to work tonight, although with people in town, Carillo might want the help. He might actually rest at a decent hour, and the girl, who was not a girl despite what Carillo called her, would thank Batch for that, which was good but another thing that made Batch want to turn around.

But it would be warm inside the hotel, and maybe there'd be some interesting news, so with a sigh, Batch stuck to her path and didn't do more than nod to anyone who called out a greeting. Most of the stage drivers knew her enough to know to leave her alone. The visitors—the well-dressed ones—didn't know her and might stare a bit or turn up their noses. It shouldn't make her stomach tight.

It did, all the same. There was no booze to dull it anymore, although the thought sounded sweet.

Batch paused outside the hotel in the light that spilled out from the open doors, then squared her jaw and pushed herself up the wooden steps and into the noise and heat from the crowd. She'd go in. She'd eat. She'd leave.

And look for Carillo.

It didn't take much to find him. He was half-perched on a stool by the bar, eyes on the room, on the strangers and the servers at the tables and, often, on the woman in the dark dress who sat at one of the tables, the one closest to the far window, and played cards whenever strangers were in town, as though ladies did that.

That lady did, anyway, and didn't seem to care about the other ladies, the ones passing through, who sneered or looked reproachful or took their meals in their rooms so as not to encounter women who gambled or liked a good time or were paid to like a good time. Ruby de la Tour, which was the name the girl gave and the name everyone used, sat at her table and dealt hands, and won or lost, and charmed just about everyone she talked to, including Carillo, who wasn't charmed by anybody.

Ruby was for her reddish hair, maybe; Batch had never dared ask. Ruby's dresses were not as costly as those others, but neither were they glittering and beribboned as the good-time girls' things. Ruby dressed nearly like a schoolteacher, but in softer fabrics with more color, and with jewelry that, made of paste or not, sparkled.

Carillo looked at her often, crinkles forming at the corners of his dark eyes, as if he wanted to smile but wasn't going to, not in front of others. For the first few weeks Ruby had been in the area, he had simply called her, "the girl." Tinney had cackled each time he heard it. Batch, half-drowned in whiskey and listening from the corner of the hotel or outside the doors, hadn't understood.

Batch turned away from Carillo toward the bar, then turned away from that too, although there were no empty seats at any tables. Eulalia, the owner's wife, would feed Batch in the kitchen if Batch was having a bad night, but with this many people in the hotel, Batch would likely get in the cook's way. So she sighed and sidled up to the bar, near to Carillo without impeding his view, and asked Bill behind the bar for something to eat.

Then, while she was waiting, she twisted to look over the crowd, and count heads, and try to spot anyone who might be trouble. She wasn't as good at it as Carillo, but then, she'd only been doing it for a few months. Anything before then, before Batch had been Blue, had been more unofficial help than anything. A silly girl following around a man who was more or less good, and often kind, and—a word Batch didn't use but Tinney did—noble.

She'd helped then, sure, and hurt things as well, with her fists and her mouth and her drinking. But thinking it over now, she supposed that she must've helped Carillo more than she'd fucked up, otherwise he wouldn't have bothered with her when she was at her worst.

But he had. He had faith and it made Batch's palms sweat with the thought that she might let him down again.

Brawls on rowdy nights, the occasional accusation of cheating or stealing, that was all the town had to deal with these days. The wrangle and fuss with Brannan seemed to have ended all the scheming and land-grabbing attempts from newcomers to the valley—or at least, ended all the rougher attempts. Tinney muttered darkly about lawyers and senators and money and respectability. But Brannan had been the biggest bully around, and all his hired muscle and gunpower hadn't done him much good in the end, so the rest had quieted down too. The valley belonged to the farmers now, more than likely. White farmers, anyway. Most of the old Californios had ended up like Tinney.

"Didn't I just send you home?" Carillo asked without taking his eyes from the room.

"Have to eat." Batch focused on the plate Bill set before her, digging in without any fanfare to chicken and carrots and two thick slices of buttered bread. Bill also put a cup of coffee down in front of her, with no cream or sugar, and winked when Batch nodded her thanks.

Carillo paid Batch no mind while she ate, or at least, seemed to, but when Batch was down to sopping up gravy with her bread, he tipped his head her way. "You aren't any use to anyone tired."

Batch stiffened, more for the words than his tone, which was light. A long time ago, she would have thrown a punch at him for that. And been sorry for it the next day, because he never would fight her back. She knew what he meant now, anyway. He was worried.

Ruby frowned when they talked like this, but she didn't understand yet how Batch was.

Even now, Batch looked up at Carillo just to scowl. "When I can't take it, I'll let you know," and shoved the last of her bread in her mouth.

Carillo had that almost-smiling look about him again, which made Batch return to her plate and her coffee while her cheeks went hot.

"Well, I don't need you here." Carillo reached back for the glass he'd left on the bar and had a sip from it. Batch swallowed, then downed what was left of her coffee in one painful gulp.

"I don't need to go home." Batch started up from her seat, one hand clenched reflexively, then caught sight of Ruby watching them both, mouth puckered in concern.

"Didn't say you did," Carillo replied, easy except for how now Batch had most of his attention and he wasn't trying to hide it. "You do a lot, Batch, and I'm grateful," he added, sending Batch's heart to racing and making her shoot a panicky look to Ruby, who must have told him to do this. "But someone your age should be enjoying the night off." Carillo rubbed his nose, visibly uncomfortable for a moment. "Bill is a good 'un, or so says Tin."

Carillo was about ten to fifteen years older than Batch, but hardly an old man like Tinney. Batch didn't say a word about her age or his age, however, too busy glancing wildly from Carillo, to Ruby, to the bar, where Bill was busy uncorking a bottle down at the other end. Bill was average height, with hazel green eyes and a decent mustache. He was also pale, with smooth hands, and would likely be disgusted by the mud and the filth of the loggers up around Stumptown. The mud got on everything in the rainy season. That was no place for fuss, or clean, soft hands.

Batch quickly shook her head. "No."

Carillo's sigh was relieved but not surprised. "Tin said you'd say no. But there's plenty of others to talk to."

Batch's chin was up before she could think better of it. But being clear-eyed meant at least catching any challenges before they came out of her mouth. Carillo heard them anyway, and looked at her directly, which silenced her but good.

Batch at eighteen, nineteen, twenty, used to trail after him whenever he'd been in the area. Carillo had just been a wanderer and occasional stage guard then. He wasn't much one for words and neither was she, with no one giving a single shit what crazy, oddball Batch said, but a few drinks to ease her down and she'd chatter on, annoying him, annoying everyone within earshot, probably, searching for the thing to say to make it better.

Never knew what it was then. She suspected she did now, and it was why she didn't want to go back to her room. When she did sleep, she slept deeper and more peacefully than she had in years, but when she was awake, she remembered things.

She turned to duck Carillo's stare, then resented herself for it and turned back. She cocked a hip and stood with her hand on her waist. She could fuck Bill. Batch wasn't pretty like Ruby but she knew what that wink had meant, and she doubted he would need coaxing, even with his nice manners.

But her mouth was so dry. She might have told Carillo that she hadn't done anything like that since getting her mind clear, but no way in hell was she ever going to say something like that to Mariano Carillo. He wouldn't offer pity, he never did, but he wouldn't understand.

Batch gave Carillo a teasing smile instead. "He seems the civilized kind. Do I look like I'd be somebody's wife?"

It was the wrong thing to say, somehow, even if she didn't know why. Carillo frowned and shook his head, slow and regretful. "Batch..."

"These all visitors going up to the resort?" Batch asked quickly, lowering her head. Out of the corner of her eye, she could see fine dresses and simple dresses and shades of pink and yellow that put her in mind of spring. She also saw filled glasses and empty glasses and brown and amber bottles. People were enjoying themselves and the drink. Their voices were loud, even the ladies'.

Bad night. She shouldn't have come in here.

Carillo's calm voice cut into her thoughts. "This crowd doesn't look especially inclined to start any trouble. Nothing that John couldn't handle, if it came to that." John owned the hotel and was a giant of a man. He did not enjoy fighting, but he could toss just about anyone into the street with very little effort. He'd bounced Batch a time or two, though never going so far as to throw her. Eulalia had found Batch almost immediately afterward and put her to bed in front of the kitchen stove with the dogs.

She would have put Batch upstairs if the hotel had empty beds on those nights, but Batch had been the one to protest. No use dirtying up clean linens for someone who wouldn't even thank her for it.

Batch's throat grew tight. Bad night, indeed, for her to be thinking of all the ways she'd embarrassed herself, and all the people who had seen her do it and kept her around in spite of it. But there wasn't a local who hadn't seen Batch in a brawl or begging for a drink, and Brannan trying to rattle her by reminding her of it had only set off Carillo's temper and given Batch enough stubborn, furious spite to keep herself from drinking just that much longer. One day, then two, then a horrible nightmare of a week, then another, and another.

Six months along now, and with the town somewhat peaceful, Batch had no clue what to do with herself. Tinney was worried and Carillo was worried. Ruby was probably worried and Ruby didn't know even half of the things Batch had gotten up to in her restless, fool life.

Batch curled her hands into fists, then exhaled as she relaxed them. Getting into scrapes, drinking, were not things she did anymore. She just didn't know what the hell else to do. That was part of the problem.

"Guess I'll go for a walk," she told Carillo at last, and nodded to him and then to Ruby, who had a watchful eye on Batch that Batch didn't think was out of jealousy, but wasn't sure exactly what it was out of. Concern, possibly. Ruby didn't know her like Carillo did, but she had been there in those first sober weeks, and Batch couldn't be sure what she'd seen. Batch's memory of that time was full of holes.

She remembered Carillo when she'd offered her help with Brannan and all his hired guns, and how Carillo hadn't laughed but his gaze had gone fierce, and he'd said, "Only if you're dry, Batch."

He never had called her Blue, and he'd taken her offer seriously as few others would have. It was no wonder Batch followed him, even now when she might have done anything.

She slipped out of the hotel without stopping to talk to Ruby or looking back toward the bar.

She hadn't noticed how hot it was inside the hotel until the cool night air hit her. She moved out of the way of the doors and down the wooden steps before stopping to turn her face up to the sky and the clouds just starting to trail over the half moon.

Her view was silver and blue and a glowing white, changing even while she watched, the stars twinkling in and out of sight. It wasn't like seeing sunlight behind the colored glass window of the grand church in Los Cerros, but it put her in mind of it. A freer version, for all that it was cold out and the valley was not what they called a sacred place. Batch didn't think she was meant for the city, or the church, when stars and moonlight took her breath away.

Her first real night without a drink, she remembered Carillo putting her on guard duty but taking her gun; it had been useless to her with her hands shaking and her guts twisting so hard she'd been bent in half. He could've sent her packing then. But he hadn't. And Tinney had fussed, and John and Eulalia had come by with food Batch hadn't wanted. But Batch had stayed on guard all night, sitting outside the jail while Carillo slept, looking up at the sky and sipping the beer Tinney had brought to supposedly keep her from getting even sicker.

She also remembered fucking up only a day or so later. Too weak to stand, much less keep watch. The others didn't blame her, but she did. They'd had to bring in outsiders to help. Why that should rankle more than her many other failures, she didn't know. Smooth and calm and clean outsiders, who'd watched Batch like the others, as if they knew her, as if they cared. And Batch had snarled, and been sorry for it, and said sorry for it, or at least dreamed she had.

She'd fallen asleep to singing, one of those nights. Joined in the singing a few nights later, her voice strained and weak. But the music had been a nice distraction. Something from those days that wasn't terrible, like the memory of Tinney and Hooper smiling.

Cigar and cigarette smoke drifted out from the hotel and the shadows nearby. The lamplight from bare windows and what moonlight there was caught on a few spangles from beaded dresses and costume jewelry. Soft laughter came and went, in high and low registers, which meant girls flirting, or working, in the dark with those passing through.

Batch had never been much good at flirting. Even in a red dress and stockings, no one had led her to any secret places to whisper in her ear or give her the trinkets that some girls had collected like prizes. Maybe they would have if she'd known how to react to such things. Maybe she should have let those girls teach her, but she'd been restless by then, missing the sky and the moon and Carillo.

She wished those girls well and these girls too, and considered walking back this way in a while to make damn sure they were well, and turned her attention pointedly away from a patch of a red shirt and the spark of a cigarette at the corner of the building next door, where the light was too dim to see much else.

She walked on, away from the hotel and her side of town, thinking about the girls, and Ruby, who was a widow and gambled or served drinks for a living, but had probably done other things. She'd marry again someday, Batch suspected, because Carillo didn't care about a person's past the way some did, and because the town was becoming respectable, and getting married something done by respectable folk.

She wondered if Carillo had considered the notion yet, and thought not, although Tinney might have considered it for him.

It must be about the nicest thing in the world to have a someone like that, a for sure person, who thought only good about you no matter how much of a mess you might have been, and promised to stay with you and never go until death parted you. Someone like that, well… Batch had nothing for someone like that except scarred fists and a single room.

That was probably what Tinney meant when he told Batch to go out and learn to do something.

Batch knew how to do lots of things. It was just that other people could also do them, or she had no need to do them now, living in town like she did. She could cook as well as sew, although her sewing was not fine enough for her to work for a dressmaker. She could hunt food with a rifle, and dress it too. Shuffle cards. Sing, if not well. Her baking was not something she had a lot of practice with, save for biscuits. She could hit a target with a pistol, although not dead center like some sort of gunslinger, and grind coffee, and repair some leather, and braid rope. Chop wood. Fish from the river. Help style a girl's hair. She even had a distant memory of kneeling in the dirt and helping her mother plant beans when she couldn't have been more than five years old.

Tinney meant it for her to have interests that weren't whiskey and all the roads whiskey led her down. Or maybe he meant it so she wouldn't wind up like him; a farmer with no farm and no plan except to help Carillo.

Tinney was, as usual, smarter than most people thought.

He would stop to look at a colored glass window, or a night sky of trailing clouds.

Carillo likely wouldn't, occupied with real matters. Batch hadn't ever considered that before.

Six months with clear eyes meant considering a great deal she hadn't ever considered before. There was a future in front of her, and she didn't know what was in it, except that there wouldn't be no wedding. She had only really tried to stay with anyone twice, and the first had been Carillo, who had never looked her way with that sort of interest, and the second had been a visitor who had been nice, and whom Batch had followed out of the valley to see what nice was like.

She'd prowled there, too, used to wandering and also used to being told to go when her temper or the drink made her prickly and pick fights—although maybe she hadn't picked them. She would have said so after having been called a wildcat too many times, but now she wondered what Tinney would have to say about it. Probably something about how being called names and insulted over and over was like to make anyone lash out or dive into a bottle, or, in Tinney's case, retreat into books.

The idea made Batch's throat so tight that her breath rasped in and out of her, and she had to take a moment to compose herself once she reached the jail.

She called out before entering since Tinney could be jumpy about surprises, but the small front room with the stove and the desk and the solitary chair was empty. The stove was cold, with not even old coffee in the pot. Batch poked her head around the back to check the two cells, but the doors were swinging open, the cots within unoccupied.

Carillo must really not be expecting any trouble, even with so many visitors in town, if he'd sent Tinney off for a break too. Unless Tinney would be back soon. If that happened, maybe he'd be in the mood to talk, or listen, not that Batch had any particular words in mind to say.

She went to get fresh water for the pitcher in the back and to make a new pot of coffee if she felt like it, rustled around in the desk for cards or dice or something to do and found only a dime novel that didn't belong there. She lit the stove, and then a lamp to take with her, and finally rolled a cigarette, which she sparked on the stove before going into the back to get comfortable on one of the cots in the cells.

She leaned back, resting her head against the wall and bending a knee to rest her arm while the smoke rose and curled and disappeared. Someone moved down the alley outside, soaked in liquor and singing to himself. Batch made a face and reached for the cup left in the cell, using it for her ashes. Then she leaned back again, searching for the peace she used to get after a few rounds, until even that hadn't worked anymore.

The drinking had been worse in those last months of it. Even she'd known that at the time. People had assumed she'd had her heart broken when she'd been out there in the wide world, but Batch's heart had never been a part of it. Or if it had, she hadn't known it; she'd felt no blushes, no butterflies.

She didn't feel them now, either, even though Carillo would marry, and the town would get a mayor or some other nonsense, and the churches would be more than some tents up in the hills or the brick building about fifteen miles out, and nobody was going to allow a female deputy if Batch even wanted to be one.

Huh. She was more worried about that than having to watch Carillo tie the knot.

Tobacco mingled with the faint scent of lavender and the woodsmoke scent that had sunk into the blankets, which was a damn sight better than what they could have smelled like. Batch took a deep breath and let her eyes close.

A quiet creak of leather had her sitting up and putting a hand on her gun before her eyes were fully open, only for her to freeze in surprise. At herself, at Hooper, who stood in the doorway that led from the front to the back. Hooper was nearly drawn down too because Batch was, and Batch had no cause to be as jumpy and nervous as Tinney, but she hadn't expected a visitor, and certainly not Hooper.

She was maybe also surprised to recognize Hooper at all. Batch's memories of the events of six months ago were patchy at best. Hooper hadn't even been in town for longer than a few weeks, Batch had been weak and sick for much of that time.

But she was unmistakable, somehow. Maybe it was her height. Hoop—as Carillo called her, Hooper, to Tinney and Batch and everyone else, although Tinney had happened to pass on that her given name was Olivia—was taller than most women and some men.

Maybe it was her hair, cut shockingly short and parted off-center, then pomaded to make the dark waves shine, as if Hooper was fine with attention.

Or maybe it was that she was one of the few other women Batch had ever seen who habitually wore pants.

Batch glanced down to them, and then to the holster Hooper proudly strapped to her thigh because unlike Batch, Hooper wanted people to know she knew how to use that gun. Batch finally flicked her gaze up, startled all over again to realize how young Hooper was, or looked, all tanned and freckled skin, clear as a mountain stream, eyes deep blue like the midday sky. Her red checkered shirt looked new. She could've stepped down from the bandbox at a city parade except for the gun. And the pants.

Then Hooper quirked a smile before holstering crossing her arms and leaning against the doorjamb. She crossed her arms, still smiling. "Batch," she said easily, "didn't mean to scare you."

Hooper said everything easily, did everything easily. Batch had forgotten that. Insults and trouble slid from Hooper's shoulders like snow melting in the sun. As far as Batch knew, once all the trouble with Brannan had died down, Hooper had left town as quietly as she'd come. Batch didn't even know why Hooper had stopped to help Carillo in the first place, since Hooper had been quick to tell people that her father had taught her to mind her own business and her mother had raised her to fight only when necessary.

Something that made no sense when Batch considered how good Hooper was with that pistol, and a rifle, and the way Tinney said she'd knocked out some hired tough.

Batch blinked several times, then met eyes of deep water blue and took her hand off her gun before she could embarrass herself more. "Hooper," she returned the greeting, her voice oddly high.

She'd dropped her cigarette, which thankfully hadn't singed the blanket much. Batch picked it up for a final drag, then stubbed it out in the cup.

"I wasn't scared," she heard herself say, as though she had to explain herself. "Not of you, I mean. I know you're... well, Tinney vouches for you."

She glanced up. Hooper wasn't exactly smiling, but there was a hint of it at the corner of her pink mouth.

"I'll take that reference with pride," she returned, voice husky. She could not have been more than two and twenty. Batch wondered how long she'd been out on her own, working like she did, to be so confident and still look so young. Too confident, likely.

But then again, choosing to dress like that, to wear her hair short, brought attention, a whole different kind than the thick curves under her men's clothing would. Hooper knew how to handle herself. She was as controlled as Carillo, maybe more so.

Her parents must be something remarkable.

Batch didn't ask about them. Didn't do anything but swallow dryly and let her heart slow down while she debated offering the kid coffee, although she couldn't have explained the urge. She wasn't sure about unfamiliar company, if Hooper could be called that.

Batch hadn't laid eyes on Hooper since those days, although Hooper could have been around. Batch walked the town or sat up all night on duty in the jail or went home, but she'd avoided most anything else. People who had known her before were difficult to face. Hooper, who had never met Blue but had witnessed Batch falling apart, was only slightly better.

Hooper carried herself like a character in that dime novel, all skill and sense. It was no wonder Carillo had accepted her offer to help despite not knowing her at the time.

Batch met Hooper's eyes again, which were darkly fringed, the lashes the same color as her hair, making her eyes startlingly bright. Batch's hair wasn't nearly so dark. Her eyes were simply brown, not even especially warm or deep. She thought, faintly, of someone once praising the dark freckle beneath her left eye and shape of her mouth, but that had been a long time ago, and from a liar, and she didn't know why the memory would come to mind now.

"So, Batch," Hooper began, and Batch heard herself jump into jerky speech.

"You riding guard with the group heading up to the springs?" Batch had heard a lot about Hooper's work choices from Tinney. Tinney liked to talk and probably thought Batch hadn't been listening. "That's a risk.

Only thing riskier would be riding guard on a mail coach." Mail coaches were full of mail—and money.

Hooper raised her eyebrows, then rolled a shoulder in a sort of a shrug. "Got to make a living somehow. But it's harder to sneak up on me then you'd think. No one's done it yet." A grin would have been cocky. Hooper didn't quite go that far, but she did smile. "You got any more tobacco?"

Batch narrowed her eyes, but tossed Hooper her pouch. She fell back against the wall and considered Hooper's hands, which were probably rough from work but didn't look it. They were clean, as if Hooper had scrubbed up for her night in town. Batch last remembered noticing them when Hooper had been strumming a guitar and singing. She'd been playing older songs, songs she seemed too young to know. Batch wondered again about her family, and who had let someone so young out into the dangerous world all by herself.

Hooper looked up, her gaze sly like she knew exactly what Batch was thinking. Without looking away, she bit the pouch string to pull the pouch closed before tossing it onto the bed next to Batch. Then she dragged her tongue across the paper and slid the rolled cigarette in and out of her mouth to seal it. She lit a match on the wall, the light flaring in front of her eyes while sending the rest of the room's shadows in all directions.

"Carillo is over at the hotel. So's the girl, I mean Ruby, if you wanted to say hello," Batch offered, shifting a little on the bed. Hooper might enjoy silence, but even though she was sober, Batch suddenly wanted to fill it. She frowned when Hooper flicked the used match into the cup Batch has used for her ashes, more alarmed than impressed at Hooper's aim, but sat up to hold the cup out for Hooper's use.

"I know. Spoke to them already. Tinney too. I always do when I stop by." Hooper was not exactly stingy with words, but wasn't handing them out all at once either. Carillo likely loved that. Batch thought of Hooper singing and was confused and then annoyed at being confused.

Batch frowned again, or had never stopped. "You've been by since then?"

Hooper left the doorway to come take the cup from her, but didn't step into the cell to join Batch on the cot. "Did you think I'd left you?" She looked down at the red tip of her cigarette, then up again quickly. "I came back. Please don't frown."

Batch rubbed her forehead with her thumb as if that would wipe the unhappy furrow away, although why her displeasure should make any difference to Hooper was beyond her.

Hooper waited a beat, then gave Batch a smile more careful than her last one. "You look different cleaned up."

That sounded like Carillo out to prod Batch into taking better care of herself.

Batch jerked her chin up and parted her lips to let some angry words fly out, only to get trapped in Hooper's wide, bottomless eyes, shining clear like Hooper only said what she meant.

Batch was too inclined to find insult, too used to finding insult, that she forgot that some folks offered none.

"Ah." She lowered her hand to her cheek, then her lap. "Without stable muck on my face or bent over to be sick, you mean?" She flicked a glance up, only half-kidding.

Hooper blinked and borrowed some of Batch's frown. "Just different," she answered at last, quietly. "Still—" she waved loosely toward Batch, possibly gesturing to her pants and men's getup, being the only notable things about Batch. "You look good," she added firmly. "But still tired. I'd hoped you wouldn't still be so tired."

The words dug into Batch's chest. She was tired. More from thinking than from lack of sleep, but there was some of that, too. She considered offering up another joke, choosing to remark on her clothes instead of anything else. Of course she looked the same; she didn't know how to dress right the other way, other than stockings and trying to show off what little breasts she had. But in the end, she quirked a smile and said, "I could try to get fancy, put some pomade in my hair."

Then she made a show of curving back into the wall. "Maybe some ribbons," she added, feeling silly. "Or a comb inlaid with mother-of-pearl."

Hooper didn't look offended. Her whole expression brightened, and she gave Batch a half-moon of a smile in return before scratching the bridge of her nose.

"Might look good at that." Hooper was water flowing over rocks as she leaned against one side of the bars and puts her smoke to her lips like she'd done it all her life. Her smile stayed put.

Batch's chin went up again without reason or her say so.

"Men used to like that kind of thing," she informed Hooper, though she should've kept quiet. "'Course, didn't much matter about all that, it turns out. They weren't fussy, and neither was I if they bought me a drink." It was worse than poking a bruise. It made her squirm inside and out and move on the cot so she didn't have to meet Hooper's eyes even though Hooper hadn't made Batch say anything. It was just... Batch remembered now, so many things she wished she didn't. The parts that Tinney kindly ignored and Carillo would not mention directly. Hooper would have no reason to know about them, unless she'd seen Batch before at some point, in the logging camps or somewhere else.

Batch hoped not. Though here she was talking about it for no damn reason, bringing it out into the open. Some still called her Blue when they came into the valley.

She cleared her throat and pretended she hadn't said anything. "I'd look ridiculous and everyone knows it. You'd know it if—how old are you anyway?" A fool question, as well as rude, and one Hooper was probably asked in every town from here to Los Cerros. "Sorry," Batch offered immediately, turning back toward Hooper. "Turns out even sober, I talk a lot of bullshit."

Hooper seemed to remember she held a cigarette and took a pull. "Just how old do I have to be?" she asked, exhaling. She wasn't annoyed. She wasn't anything but watchful and far too controlled. It was like when Batch had been a kid, looking up into the goddamned face of fate, only it was not the hard-as-granite Mariano Carillo scowling down at her. Hooper smiled. "I'd say I'm old enough."

Batch had never smiled at anyone like that, even at her youngest and prettiest. She'd seen a few, ignored them or hadn't understood them or run from them. She'd been busy, anyway, following Carillo around or getting herself into scrapes.

Her stomach twisted. Her heart was racing. She glanced down at her hands, expecting to see them shaking and useless again, or to wake up bottle-achy and dry-mouthed on a saloon floor. She swallowed, but though her throat was dry, she wasn't thirsty, not like that.

"I don't..." Her voice was hoarse. She decided she'd been mistaken about the smile. "I don't remember much of what we said, then, if we said anything. You probably told me before."

Hooper could go as unreadable as Carillo or Ruby at the card table. But she nodded slowly. "I did. But I don't mind telling you again. I'm twenty-four." She actually seemed delighted when Batch lifted her head to regard her doubtfully. "I just look younger. I get that from my mother—my height too. You liked hearing that for some reason. I think I told you all about my mother at some point...." She stopped, and swept her gaze over Batch's face, which was probably pale with shame. She gentled her voice. "I don't mind telling you that again, either, if you want."

Batch exhaled and unfurled her hands, which she'd clenched on her knees. "I'm sure you didn't come here to tell me stories about your mama." Which was almost asking why Hooper was there, although Batch did not want to do that. It was close to asking how badly off Batch must have been back then to have Hooper, practically a stranger, so worried about her even now.

Silence followed.

Batch fiddled with the tobacco pouch without opening it. "Was it to say hello?" That was the most likely reason, unless Hooper had left behind that dime novel and come looking for it, only to find Batch here. Batch turned back toward Hooper, catching Hooper with her head up and her eyes closed, inhaling through her nose. Hooper blinked slowly several times when she saw Batch watching her.

"Hello?" she echoed, as though she genuinely didn't know what Batch was talking about.

"Since you haven't seen me," Batch prompted, only to hear herself. Hooper had not been looking for her. Batch went hot around the collar, then warm in the face. She shrugged despite her blushes.

"I did try, and it's not a bad place to visit. Not home, but not bad." Hooper dropped what was left of her smoke to crush it out with her boot, then bent down to pick up the remnant and toss it into the cup. "It's probably good that you were busy." She paused to balance the cup on one of the cross bars. "You're not staying at the hotel like Carillo does."

It was an observation, but Batch took it for a question. "I have a room on the other side of town."

Hooper turned toward her and Batch looked up, straight into Hooper's eyes, and felt her blush grow hotter, curling through her like steam from a bath.

"I'd like to see it," Hooper held her gaze, speaking softly and with a care Batch only vaguely noticed, "if you've a mind to show me."

The streets around the jail were quiet enough now that Batch could hear noise from further on, likely from the cantina, where they often played music. She smoothed her hands down her thighs, as if her palms were damp, and frowned without moving her gaze away like she ought to. But Hooper was watching her, thoughtful about it, like Carillo but also like Hooper, with those eyes like deep water, as if it all meant something.

Which it must, if Batch was sweating and her stomach was knotted tight with uncertainty. Sometimes people made statements that sounded like offers, but which were really about nothing at all. A girl in that house down south had once offered to lend Batch her earrings and put them on her. Didn't mean anything. Or might not have. Batch had… Batch had been drunk, but not drunk enough to look someone in the eye who wanted her despite what she was.

She'd started talking. She always started talking. Then drinking. Then she'd run.

Batch hadn't meant her remark for an invitation. She didn't think she had. She didn't think anything except that her throat was awfully dry. She also wasn't running, or telling Hooper to get along home, wherever that was; Batch probably knew, she just didn't remember.

"Maybe some other night." Hooper inclined her head politely, easily, maybe would have tipped her hat if she'd had one.

That made Batch frown again, but sober, she made no sense anyway. "You're in town that long?" She was barely loud enough to be heard over the distant music.

Hooper was no longer looking at her. "Few days is all," she explained, gesturing. "Take 'em up to the waters. Take some down from the waters." She was back in the doorway, although Batch somehow had not noticed her move. "I'm glad you're doing better."

Batch wanted to bristle, but her mind was too full of too many other things to bother with any prickling. She swallowed. "Me too."

Hooper stopped and twisted around to give her another smile, this one full and brilliant, as if all of her smiles were like the moon. "See you around, Batch."

She didn't make a sound as she left.

Two

BATCH must have been confused. That's what she nearly decided, except that Batch was sober, so lying to herself was harder than it used to be.

She didn't return to her room. She rolled a few cigarettes, one after another, and left them in the front room for Tinney, sparing him the trouble, since his hands ached when the weather was cold. Then she stood watch over an empty jail until her eyes shut on their own. Tinney must have limped in at some point and left her there, eventually falling asleep too. His snores woke her around dawn, and she couldn't go back to sleep.

She was out of tobacco and cranky by mid-morning, but she wandered to the hotel, pulling at her coat and rumpled shirt. The town was changed by daylight. People that didn't visit the hotel for evening entertainment gave her the eye and she was tired enough to think about sneering back at them. She nodded greetings instead, because she was learning, and went inside to shovel beans and bread and coffee into her mouth until she was stuffed.

The main room was empty of everyone but some girls doing the cleaning. Neither of the coaches destined for the hot springs resort had left, and John wasn't sure they would, with the way some of the gentlemen had bent their elbows at the bar all night. Batch doubted that was part of the cure the men were supposed to be taking, but thanked John for the information and slipped outside in time to nearly run smack into Carillo.

Of course, he was up when he should have been in bed. He might have been on his way there; Batch didn't ask. He gave her a glower that said she looked as tired as he felt, and Batch made a face and walked on by him anyway. It was her shift and she was going to take it. Brannan had lost all respect and most of the backing of the other ambitious landowners in the area, but he did still have a few friends, and it paid to be cautious.

She stayed mostly around the stables not attached to the hotel, or at the blacksmith's, down and away from the center of their little no-name town. She talked to one new visitor riding in, borrowed some tobacco from the stable hand, and ended up mostly staring at the mess of hay in the back of the stables that Blue would have used as a mattress, more nights than not. There was nothing to do, which was a good sign for the people in town, but the sunlight snuck through the stable roof, hardly blocked at all, reminding Batch of the nights she'd slept in the rain. One of the hired coaches left around noon, full of ladies impatient to be away. The other stayed behind.

Batch stunk of smoke and sweat by the time the sun started to drop, and although it was her usual day and Eulalia was probably expecting her, she asked the blacksmith's kid to run over to the hotel for her to request hot water for a bath.

A short while later, Batch followed the sound of conversation back to the St. Christopher, and slipped between the swinging entrance doors. She passed her eye over the locals by the bar for a beer after work, and the visitors who, feeling the effects of their revelry or not, seemed intent on reliving the night before, until she spied the tall, familiar form resting in a chair at Ruby's elbow.

Hooper had cards in her hands, but she and Ruby didn't seem to be much interested in them. Hooper was talking, and Ruby was nodding but grinning faintly, as if something was funny to her and her alone. When it looked like Ruby was about to turn and see Batch standing there, moongazing at the two of them, Batch hurried on to the stairs.

The bath water was warm by now, not hot, but still agreeable. Batch didn't waste time and unpinned her hair to get it wet, and used all the rose-scented soap Eulalia left out for her to get her skin and hair squeaky clean.

Lingering to smell the roses in her hair would be a fool thing to do, which might have been why she did it, but there was no around to notice except Ana, there to take towels and leave towels and straighten the room, and Ana didn't care about Batch squeezing her hair as dry as she could get it, or admiring the embroidered green leaves on the hem of the handkerchief someone had left behind, or daydreaming over the selection of perfumes and powders on the table in the ladies' bath room.

Batch didn't use any of that stuff, just finished drying off before putting her clothes back on. She combed her hair out and patted it with the towel one last time before twisting it and pinning it up at the back of her head. The damp, warm air made wisps curl over her forehead and around her ears, almost as if she'd arranged them. In the mirror, color was high on her cheeks. The reflection only showed her head and shoulders, Tinney's kerchief around her neck where Batch had used to tie a black or emerald ribbon when she'd been working. She imagined it there now and knew it was not the heat bringing the color to her face.

Turning away at last, she hesitated over her belt and gun, but rather than leave it with Ana and give the girl something else to keep track of, Batch tied the holster on and then, taking a deep breath, left the room.

It was beginning to get lively, although not as much as the night before. That explosion of partying had quieted them some, and most paid Batch no mind as she walked among them. Batch was the one glancing from left to right, almost wishing one of them would start trouble, all the while wondering at the sweat-dampness of her palms even though she'd just bathed. It was worrisome enough to make her pause at the foot of the stairs, and then, when she felt herself being observed, she turned and answered Ruby's waved invitation without thinking.

She walked over to Ruby's table with her throat tight and her step quick. She wiped her palms on her coat before she sat down.

The table's taller occupant did not startle, but Batch got the impression that Hooper knew who had arrived.

"Evening." Ruby was a queen among women, a rare flower, and Carillo was a lucky son of a gun to have found someone like her, because she didn't ask how Batch was, or comment on how flushed and damp she must be, even though Batch looked like something the cat toyed with and decided not to eat. She also called over to the bar to order Batch a beer. Ruby knew Batch wouldn't really drink it, but it spared Batch from people trying to buy her a shot like in the old days, and because people were suspicious of those who drank water at a poker table. Then, even though she knew Batch was no good at it, and didn't really have money for it, Ruby dealt her into the game she and Hooper were playing.

Although, now that Batch was at the table, she noticed they were playing with matchsticks.

"Never hurts to practice," Ruby explained with a wink when Batch looked up. "Real stakes soon enough when the place fills and the voices get loud."

Batch looked over her cards for a long time before she raised her head.

"Hooper." Her voice didn't shake. That was something.

"Roses?" Hooper asked, wide-eyed, then blinked and picked up the mostly untouched glass at her elbow to take a sip. She swallowed. "Hey, Batch."

Hooper sipped whiskey like somebody who knew better to get drunk when playing cards, even when playing for matchsticks. She'd probably work on that same whiskey for hours. Maybe she was just smart. Maybe she didn't think about the state of peace of so many others looked for inside a bottle. Maybe she had more control than that. Or maybe she just didn't like the taste.

Some people didn't need a drink to do things. Batch didn't either, exactly, but it had made a lot of things easier.

Or seemed to, she heard in Tinney's voice. She had no argument for him there. Truthfully, she couldn't imagine Hooper needing drunk courage. She had too much of it to begin with.

"It's rose soap," she answered Hooper's question belatedly, although all Batch could smell was the drinks, including the beer Esperanza, Eulalia and John's daughter, brought over to her.

Ruby smiled widely when Batch looked up, but only remarked on the resort's increased business, and how a clever person interested in that sort of thing could make money by offering guests something other than the hot springs to visit. She didn't say if she was planning to be that clever person, or how, but Hooper jumped in with talk of the stuff the health tourists got up to on their trips to the geysers, and it spared Batch from having to say anything for a while.

She didn't usually spend a lot of time in the hotel when business picked up. Not these days.

Carillo walked past twice, first heading in to talk to John, then heading out again. He did stop for a moment, staring at the three of them until Batch raised her eyebrows and Ruby mouthed something to him. Then he nodded to Batch and to Hooper before giving Ruby a not-quite smile. There were lines at the corners of Carillo's eyes, sun lines, worry, lines from age. In all the time Batch had known him, she'd never thought they could also be from smiling.

Ruby was practically giddy with it all, even after Carillo slipped out. "It's good to have us together again," she announced in a decided way, "without all the...." She fluttered a hand to indicate, apparently, all of the affairs and skirmishes concerning Brannan.

Ruby was in scarlet and black tonight. She tended to wear a black skirt with different jackets, perhaps to save money. She didn't put up her hair with much fuss, but she wore rings and necklaces that she never, ever gambled away. The color in her face was not rouge. She had lines at her eyes too, but a plump, curving body that did not speak of much labor. She did help around the hotel sometimes, usually at the bar, but her hands were likely soft. Her jacket was fully buttoned, her shirt pressed; nothing of her throat or chest was visible.

Batch tore her gaze from the bit of sparkle Ruby had around her neck tonight before she could get called out for staring, but that left her to look only at her cards or at Hooper.

She'd never sat with Hooper before, not that she could recall, not like this, awake and aware of so many things. The hotel was well-lit. Hooper had a faint tint of copper in her hair. Like Batch, her top shirt buttons were undone. Unlike, Batch, she had changed into a clean shirt, blue nearly as dark as midnight, with a kerchief, white with specks of paler blue, twisted and tied loosely around her neck.

There wasn't a hint of sweat on her. Even the waves of her short hair were neat and in place. She'd parted it more to one side than the other, leaving one ear exposed. Scar tissue, pink and silvery, ran along the top of the shell of her ear. It didn't look recent. All of kinds of things might have happened to cause it. Children in particular loved to get into careless scrapes. Batch frowned over it anyway, at least until Hooper turned to her, eyebrows lifted in question.

Batch stared back at her cards, because the way Hooper's lips curved made her suspect that Hooper somehow knew her heart was racing. Which was nonsense and impossible.

They played two more hands for matches, then Ruby tutted and swept the matchsticks aside. She did, after all, need to make a living. To support her—it never hurt to have another body at the poker table—and because there were still words trapped in Batch's tight throat, Batch stayed.

She stayed long enough for her skin to cool and dry, and for some others to join them. One, apparently, to try to earn back what he'd lost last night. Batch had no skill at cards, but she could tell Ruby had that fellow easily, and Batch as well, and that Hooper played pretty good for someone with such clear eyes. She was hard to read despite all that, or maybe on account of it, and it didn't take long before she and Ruby managed to drive off the first few other players.

Batch was also seriously considering leaving despite the nerves keeping her still; she would need rent money if she didn't want to end up back in a pile of wet hay.

With the table just the three of them, Ruby and Hooper started to talk like old friends again, leaving Batch to wonder what exactly had happened while she'd been sweating out every drink she'd had in her life.

"Surprised to see the kid gambling," she heard herself say after the sound of their shared laughter died down. They both turned toward her.

Hooper's eyes were wide again, disbelieving, but then a slow smile softened her mouth.

"I can play all right." Hooper's tone was warm, not insulted. "I can speak for myself too, if you wanted to talk to me directly, Batch."

Batch huffed, even though Hooper's light air made her be light in return. "Didn't your daddy teach you not to sass people?" Her big mouth never let her stay out of anything, not for long. There was a name for what she was doing, and thinking of it made her rub a hand across her lips, wanting to mash the fool things together.

Hooper's smile become a grin. "And to respect my elders too."

Ruby let out a rich laugh. Not even the look Batch directed at her would shame her into quiet. Nothing would.

Hooper leaned in to rest her elbows on the table, and that was where Batch's eyes went next, before being drawn back up to Hooper's face.

"My father taught me a lot of things, like, 'You'll win and you'll lose, no matter who you are. But when you find something good, you should try your best to keep it—or make it want to keep you.'"

Hooper had bright eyes, impossibly bright, lit like stage lights.

Batch's throat was dry. "That's cards."

"That's life." Hooper angled her chin up, her posture just a hair short of challenging. Her hands were still in view. "Huma—people get into trouble because they're afraid of losing."

"Maybe all some people do is lose," Batch said without thinking, then frowned and looked away, down at the beer she hadn't touched, as if that was to blame. She cleared her throat, pretending their silence wasn't from shock or pity. "Sounds like your pa and Carillo had the same schooling. My pa taught me..." She swallowed. "He taught me to shoot, and to make coffee, and what to do when you've spent all your wages at the bar."

"Oh, Batch, honey," said Ruby, with a hiccup in her voice.

Hooper lowered her head, tapped the side of her glass, then pushed it to the side before looking up. "But he tried to take care of you, in his way?"

Batch should never have opened her mouth. She nodded, just once.

Hooper gave her a small, gentle smile. "Then I can like him for that." She glanced to Ruby after several moments of Batch staring at her, too choked to manage words. "Another thing my father taught me was to be the best you that you can be, whatever best means to you, so that you can take care of the things you love, when you find 'em. It's really... really more of a way of life, I suppose. It's the way they are on that side of the family."

"The best you?" Ruby repeated, confused.

Batch considered Hooper's coat and vest and pants, and the hat resting on an empty part of the table. "And he had nothing to say about..." She gestured to indicate Hooper's clothing choices.

Hooper leaned back, which really only served to remind anyone looking that she had curves beneath that shirt and vest. "He says for me to be the best me. So that's what I am, what I try to be."

"Where exactly are your people from again?" Ruby asked delicately, which drew Hooper's attention away from Batch, albeit slowly.

"It's a bit of journey to get there, but we like it that way. New folks are welcome, of course, but anybody who'd mind about something as insignificant as a person's clothes is usually shown the door—so to speak. We don't run them out on a rail, you understand, but we prefer people who mind their own damn business about things like that."

Batch heard the fondness in Hooper's voice and believed her, even while knowing such a place could not exist.

Ruby said something else. Hooper answered that, too, practically glowing at the chance to talk about her home. Batch had to wonder what the hell she was doing here, then. Ruby must have as well.

"Then whyever did you leave?" she asked.

"Ah, well...." Hooper leaned in again, glancing to Batch before she began her story. "My mother's people have... a tradition... about a funny feeling, like destiny, or fate, if they meet a person they are meant for." Batch frowned at the idea of destiny, which wasn't to be found in a logging camp or by the back door of a hotel. Hooper glanced at her again, as if needing to make sure Batch was listening. "Not everyone has or wants someone, which is important to mention, but they all believe in the idea." She held Batch's gaze. "Some of them know it to be true."

"How?" Batch asked, only to grow warm all over again at the breathless quality to her voice.

Hooper answered her seriously. "They feel it." But she turned toward Ruby and lightened her tone. "Now, my father's family has something similar. Only with them, it's as I said, when they find something good. Or, as my aunt puts it, 'When it feels right, you'll know.' To them that's a place, or a person, or even a calling or a craft."

"That's just a family legend," Ruby scoffed playfully. Maybe her family had a legend too.

Batch looked over. "And your parents, they were each other's… feeling?" Never in her whole life had she looked at something and known it was right, except possibly when she'd met Carillo.

Hooper seemed pleased that Batch had asked. "Where it gets good is when they met each other. Here they are, both of them, feeling this rightness in their hearts, but of course they don't tell one another that. That would sound too fantastic to a stranger, they each thought. And, I should tell you, there are a lot like my family in our town, so they know to be patient with newcomers and outsiders who might not know or believe in these feelings."

"So each was courting the other, waiting for their chance to tell them?" Ruby clapped her hands together. "That's the sweetest thing I ever heard. It's pure hogwash and I don't believe you for a second, Olivia Hooper, but it's sweet as can be."

"Ruby, ma'am, I swear on my life, they would tell you the same if you spoke with them." Hooper grinned, but it slipped slowly from her face as she returned her eyes to Batch. "A kind of rightness in your heart."

Batch thought she ought to turn away. Surely, it would be in her expression what she thought of such an idea, ridiculous though it was, and Hooper was going to tease her, or say she was only having a small joke at their expense, telling a tale.

Batch did look down, finally, when Esperanza came around to tell Ruby something, and she remembered that others in the room could see her gazing starry-eyed at Hooper for telling a story.

"What has any of that got to do with you leaving your town?" That had been the reason for all this talk of destiny and hearts and rightness.

Hooper lowered her voice, as if she didn't want anyone else but Batch and possibly Ruby to hear this part. "I love where I grew up, but I'd met pretty much everyone there was to meet, and I didn't have that feeling. So I decided, since I wanted it, that I should go look for it, and see some of the world while I was at it. Maybe that was all I would find, but at least I'd know that I looked. Anyway, how else can you learn things without experiencing them? How else am I supposed to be more prepared to take care of someone and love them if I haven't seen so much of what there is to see? I suppose it helps me be better, too. The Olivia I was when I left is not the Olivia I am now, and I'm not mad about it."

Like it was easy to say, or do, or to think that way, Hooper shrugged at the end of all that and flashed a brief smile that Batch couldn't describe with any words she knew. That was what made her pause instead of scowling and picking a fight to cover up the fact that she understood something of what Hooper was talking about.

Batch didn't know if she liked who she was now, although she liked her better than Blue. But she hadn't set out on any kind of mission like Hooper had. She wasn't trying to find the best version of herself, for any reason. She was just trying to get by.

But then, Hooper had that odd scar, and she walked with a gun, and used her fists along with her brains, so it couldn't have been an easy journey, no matter how she carried herself.

"You all right, Batch?" Ruby asked in concern. "You're not the chattiest, but you're usually less taciturn than Carillo." Ruby used words like that, taciturn. Hooper glanced over to her as though she used them too. Maybe she'd had proper schooling in that town of hers.

"You had people and you left them?" Batch asked Hooper quietly, not really certain what to make of that, or why Hooper would grow so serious.

"For a while."

"To come here?" Batch wondered doubtfully. There was beauty in the wild places, but there were fewer and fewer of those left. "And you ended up in Carillo's mess?" Well, Brannan's mess, but everyone had looked to Carillo for help with it.

Hooper's shrug this time did not look easy. It looked cagey.

Batch narrowed her eyes. "No one ever did explain to me how you came to be involved. Was that was to spare my feelings?"

Hooper, who bluffed with a straight face and hadn't touched her drink, abruptly sat back and crossed her arms and glanced around the room. "I fully intended to stay out of it," she insisted at last. "I was new in town, only visiting really, for work. But then Brannan's people started harassing the stage's customers."

With her face in profile, Batch could see the sweep of her eyelashes over her cheeks, and the little wisps of hair on her neck below the blunt edge of her haircut. Hooper was a pretty girl, even if she might not like it said.

Or perhaps she would. Though thinking of who she might like to say it to her was uncomfortable. Another pretty girl, likely, if Batch had understood her correctly the night before. Yet Hooper hadn't been speaking to a pretty girl then; she'd been speaking to Batch.

Batch startled when Hooper turned back to her, eyes twinkling. "But, well, things happened to change my mind."

"It was impressively stubborn of Mariano to resist asking others for help. I'm still surprised he accepted yours, Hooper." Ruby sighed dramatically. "That man needs to be saved from himself and I'm beginning to wonder how you all managed him this long." Her expression was relaxed, near to glowing as she started listing Carillo's faults, and really, not even Batch could be surprised that 'stubborn' was uttered again. "...Gets into trouble and insists that he can do it all himself." Even Ruby's frowns were lovely. "Everybody can use help from time to time. Were we supposed to watch him try to protect everyone with just two others to help him?"

Just two others, and one of those not much help at that. Tinney moved slow, and Batch had done her best, but it hadn't taken long for her to be near to useless. Setting Batch up to keep watch over the jail had been something Carillo himself could not do at the time, but which he had also to done get Batch out of the way. Carillo could have died if it hadn't been for Ruby for taking action, and Eulalia and John and a few others helping with him food and supplies and giving him news, and Hooper, for getting involved when she shouldn't have.

It was a damn fool thing to do, to stay, to fight. And still, they'd stuck. Stuck when no one would blame them for leaving, least of all Carillo or Batch.

What kind of person saw Batch like that, sweating and foul-smelling and awake through her nightmares, and then looked at her later and... asked to see her room?

The same kind of person that told stories about destiny and cut her hair short as a boy's. An odd person. A person that belonged in her little hometown, not out here. Yet here Hooper was, making friends with old Tin and Ruby and earning Carillo's respect. She was sitting there now nodding sympathetically while Ruby ranted about Carillo's propensity—another Ruby word—for finding trouble.

"Learning how to care for them, how they'll let you care for them, is so tricky," Hooper said, like one housewife to another. Except neither of them were properly wedded, or even proper. Ruby gambled and liked a drink and seemed to enjoy her time in Carillo's bed. Hooper... Hooper was all the things Hooper was, and also the kind to choose a lady-friend.

Lots of girls in the houses were like that, sought that. Batch had watched them and wondered, quite certain her rough hands would catch on satin and tear it to bits. Anyway, she was strange enough, not enough of a girl for marriage, too much of a gal-boy for anyone soft. Once, she had... once, before Hooper, she had thought someone had offered and she had considered it. A fool notion. A terrifying idea. That someone, even a girl who worked on her back in a lowly sort of house, who wore petticoats and lace and smelled of flowers, would like Batch enough to want Batch's hands on her for free. To want to lie with her after hours, when they slept with the windows covered to block out the daylight, and sit with her for meals, and be with her for the joy of her company.

Batch hadn't known what to do with that. She'd fled that job and that town and returned here to drink so much she'd... well, everyone knew what she'd done.

She put a hand to her throat and thought of the simple ribbon she'd worn for lack of jewelry, and how Ysabel had told her it was pretty on her.

Hooper was agreeing with Ruby now, or at least pretending to, glancing over to Batch every so often to share a smile, as if whatever the hell they were discussing was funny. Batch tried to keep her gaze away, but Hooper kept giving Ruby these serious looks that weren't serious at all. Batch wanted to hold her still and frown at her and demand to know what was amusing. She wanted to know why she'd stayed, not just through the danger but to help care for Batch. She wanted to snarl at her and make Hooper stop giving her fond glances as if they were friends, or take back her wistful invitation—or issue it again.

Batch took a deep breath and watched Hooper's lips shape words. They were lips of a naturally tempting color, nothing applied there. They might not even taste of whiskey, it had been so long since Hooper had touched her glass. Yet Batch swallowed and wished to wet her own.

Batch forced her gaze away, to Ruby, who must have noticed some of Batch's agitation because she arched an eyebrow. Batch rolled her shoulder to try to seem more at ease, and flicked a look back to Hooper, only to stop at finding Hooper's eyes on her.

Hooper studied her; there was possibly a better word but that was how it felt. Batch felt studied, Hooper's gaze tracing Batch's face while her eyebrows drew together. Then Hooper lifted her head just slightly and drew in a small breath. "Batch," she whispered, awed or wondering.

Batch jerked her gaze away and noticed her untouched beer. At the best of times, she disliked beer. It made her think of the days of getting sober. But now she pushed it farther aside to give herself a chance to push something.

She ought to speak. Drunk, there would have been no shutting her up. Clear-headed, she had too much on her mind and it all seemed to stick in her throat. She wasn't sure she hadn't been confused last night. She wanted Hooper to ask again. There was no reason for Hooper to do so.

It finally made Batch scowl. "I think I'm tired. No, I know I'm tired." Now the words spilled from her. "I... don't get out much anymore," she added, to Hooper without quite meeting Hooper's eyes. Her face burned at how young and foolish she must sound. "It's still difficult, and I meet people who expect me to... be who I was. You've both been wonderful. I'm sorry."

"It's all right, Batch," Ruby insisted warmly. "Get some rest, and maybe something to eat."

Batch nodded, even more embarrassed to be reminded to eat. She'd meant to do that after bathing. Instead, she'd sat here, full of silly, fluttering ideas. She stood, determined to ignore the butterflies along with her blushes, but then, like a girl with no control over herself around a potential sweetheart, glanced to Hooper.

Hooper stared at up her, mouth turned down in disappointment or, possibly, worry. Then their eyes met, and hers were so impossibly clear that it was a wonder she ever won at cards. Even Batch could see the warmth in them.

"I guess I'll head to my room," Batch said, her voice high and nervous and pointed, and then ducked her head and walked away, out of the hotel and into the cooler air to look up at the moon and catch her breath.

She was there for probably too long, head tilted up like a dog with a howl in its throat. She felt more than heard someone step close. She turned to find Carillo.

"For years, I never looked up. But it's lovely." She didn't know why she said it. Carillo, of course, squinted at her, then up at the moon, before obviously deciding Batch was doing poorly.

"You getting some rest?" He asked it in a meaningful way. "I would have sent you home this afternoon, but you would have bristled and done the opposite."

He gave Batch a minute or so to work that out and think about getting angry. She finally just pushed out a breath and nodded. Ruby complained about Carillo, but he wasn't the only one who didn't know how to ask for what he needed.

Batch glanced around the street, recognizing no one in particular in the figures in windows or walking past. Then she turned back to Carillo, grinning. "You ought to think about it, too. You're not getting any younger, you know, and Ruby's a spirited woman." She gave a whistle, earning herself a glare this time and almost enjoying it. She'd never tried teasing Carillo before. It was good.

"Get out of here." Carillo's voice was gravel on top of rocks on top of sand.

Batch was about to obey when a question from earlier stopped her. "How did Hooper end up in all this? She's too smart to be a hero."

Carillo regarded Batch squarely, picking through his answers. All he finally said was, "Try asking Hoop instead of me," before adding, only slightly softer, "Really, get some sleep, Batch."

Maybe it was proof of how tired she was, but instead of tensing up or clenching her fists, Batch smiled, surprising even herself. She walked on before the moment could get any stranger.

She needed to sleep but was too restless to lie down. Her hair was damp, making her shiver a little as she made her way down the main street. She took her time, fidgeting with her hands in her coat pockets and then out of them, fussing with her hair.

She ought to eat, but that wasn't where she'd said she was going, so that wasn't where she went. She slipped between buildings, picking her way through slop piles and the alley behind the dry goods store and the bakery owned by the miller's cousin, using the flickering light from a dozen windows lining the street. She was careful, intending to stay clean if she could help it.

She didn't hear a noise, but then she didn't expect to. For her peace of mind, she eased her hand down to her side as she turned and waited for Hooper to join her. But something was tugging at her lips, and something warm and anxious was brewing in her stomach, and at least the darkness hid whatever came over her face when she saw the tall figure a few yards away.

Hooper had her hat on, one hand free and easy, the other hooked in her belt. She didn't slow until she was closer, even though Batch rounding on her had to be unexpected.

"More clouds tonight," Hooper observed, so low not a peep would be heard in any of the rooms nearby. "But it doesn't smell of rain. Just fog, I think, and that only near dawn."

Batch glanced up, but the roofs of the buildings on either side blocked her view. "Do you often look at the sky?"

Hooper didn't seem bothered by the question. She came to a stop before answering thoughtfully. "I look up at the moon, and it usually makes a pretty picture. Out on the road, there's little else to look at, it's true, but sometimes, when I should be sleeping, I stare up at the moon, or the stars, or the clouds. Is that the answer you're looking for?"

Batch shook her head. "I'm not looking for anything. You're the one hunting for something." A funny feeling. Nonsense, yet Batch couldn't seem to forget it. "To be honest, I don't know what I'm looking for. I walk a lot. Usually at night."

"Do you want to walk now?" The offer was softer than feathers or the fur on Eulalia's silky little mouser.

Batch didn't agree, she just turned and started walking, waiting for Hooper to join her, which she did. There wasn't far to go, not unless Batch made a right to take them out of the alleyways. She kept to her route, marveling at how tight her chest felt, the way she was breathing faster. She was scared as a kid, possibly just because there was nothing to make this easier. Nothing she was going to do, anyway, although she could have asked her landlady for a tipple.

A few blocks away there was music, but the alleys only had quiet noises, scratching rats and movements in upstairs rooms. Batch's hands nearly swung together with Hooper's as they moved, brushing just once.

"That was a sweet song you sang when I was with you and Tinney in the jail," Hooper said with a lilt, pleasant and gentle.

Batch was too wound up to be soothed. "And what was that? Not sure I remember, I was most likely out of my mind at the time, or wishing I was drunk." She aimed the words at Hooper but Batch was the one with the ache in her gut to hear them. "Sorry."

Hooper ignored the apology. "Something about a pony. I don't think I've heard that one before, not like you sang it anyway. Sounded lonely." Hooper pulled in a breath. "You aren't drunk now, are you, Batch?" She was straightforward in a way even Carillo wouldn't be, her voice full of wondering and nothing else.

Batch was dead sober, but Hooper knew that, like she probably knew, or could guess, that Batch's heart was thudding against her ribcage and her skin was burning even though the air was near cold enough to raise bumps along her bare skin. She couldn't tell if Hooper felt the chill, not just with looking, so she finally ducked her head to search for some tobacco. She didn't want to smoke. She looked anyway. "No, I'm not drunk."

She was patting her vest before she remembered she was out, but then Hooper stopped, so Batch followed suit only to catch herself staring at Hooper's hands as Hooper finished tapping out some leaf onto a slip of paper. Batch's gaze kept traveling up, and like before, she watched silently as Hooper closed the bag and tucked it away. Hooper rolled her smoke with short, familiar motions, and even waiting for it, Batch was caught by surprise at the glimpse of tongue and teeth, the drag of Hooper's lips on the paper.

Without pausing, Hooper pulled the cigarette free and offered it to Batch, and Batch reached out to take it. It was warm to the touch.

Batch had her own matches but her mouth was too dry, her stomach too tight at the thought of a smoke. She slid the cigarette behind her ear, shivering as it immediately slipped through her damp hair and Hooper caught it before it could fall and fixed it for her.

Hooper pulled her hand away when she was satisfied, respectful, questioning, as though they weren't standing close now and Batch wasn't still shivering.

"My room's not far." Batch moved without waiting, not wanting to get caught leaning in and trembling like a rabbit. Behind her, Hooper took a breath and followed. The pomade in Hooper's hair had a kind of spicy scent. The tobacco scent was sharp too. Batch herself smelled of roses, which made her shiver again without knowing why.

"We're heading out. Dawn." Hooper offered, catching up to walk at Batch's side again.

"I never expected them to stay." What Batch was really saying was about as obvious as red flannel drawers and Carillo would have been tempted to knock the pathetic out of her before Batch got the opportunity to do it herself.

"Life is a funny thing..." Hooper started.

Batch cut her off, her voice too high yet also soft. "A funny feeling, you said."

Hooper's boots scraped in the dirt as she stopped abruptly, and Batch realized it was because she had stopped. She lifted her head to stare in surprise at the narrow stairs leading up to her room.

"Funny maybe isn't the word I should use, since it implies a joke where there is none," Hooper said, careful. "Queer maybe. Strong. Powerful. Sudden. There are all kinds of words I could use instead. Overwhelming. That's a good one."

"An overwhelming feeling," Batch murmured in confusion. She'd likely flee from such a thing, not head toward it.

She glanced over, though, to Hooper, who watched her in return. Then, before Batch could run away from her own place, she began to head up the steps. She moved quietly, though her landlady was dead to the world by now and no one occupied the room below hers. When she reached the top, she pushed open the door. Batch had nothing to steal, and anyway, the door only locked from the inside.

The room was dark. Batch busied herself with lighting the lamp and drawing the curtains on the tiny window, expecting Hooper to come in, but Hooper lingered in the doorway, observing everything with interest.

She didn't have much to see. The narrow bed, the wash stand, the chest of drawers with Batch's new clothes inside. Everything Batch owned now, excepting the money she kept in the safe in the hotel. But then, Hooper's things could likely fit on the back of one horse, which might be why her gaze skipped over the unpapered walls and came back to Batch. She finally stepped inside when Batch straightened but didn't speak.

"Beats a blanket spread over ground," Hooper remarked, making Batch narrow her eyes. Batch didn't, or shouldn't, need to be calmed. She'd probably done things Hooper had never heard of. But she still wasn't speaking, either.

Batch couldn't hear the music from here, and it was a hundred times quieter when Hooper closed the door behind her. Batch dipped her eyes down before tugging at the string wrapped around one thigh to keep her holster in place.

Hooper checked the lock, seeming surprised to find the key in it, but locked it with a turn of her wrist. She removed her hat, tossing it to the dresser, then leaned back against the wall, making herself comfortable and watching Batch with a faint smile on her face. It was a strangely welcome sight, having Hooper giving her glances from so short a distance.

"It's not a home." Batch said it because Hooper knew what a proper home was, even if it wasn't a big house on a hill. "I suppose your family has a place? Together, or spread throughout your town?" She tried to think of something similar, but all that came to mind was nights napping on the cot in the jailhouse, with Tinney snoring somewhere nearby.

Hooper regarded Batch seriously, as though Batch wasn't filling silence with questions about a town she'd never see. She took a deep breath and lowered her eyes and said, "It's a strange town, I suppose, to some. But it does its best to be welcoming, at least, to those who have someone to swear to them. We put a great deal of stock in feeling safe, making others feel safe. Protecting them, and ourselves."

Batch swallowed down a lump in her throat.

"Why—" A crack in her voice made Batch stop and try again. "Why would you ever come here? I know what you said, but why? Why help us? You could've just left. No one would have thought ill of you for it. This isn't your town. You had no one to protect here."

"You ask that like it's been bothering you," Hooper said, tender, then left no time for a reply. "Maybe I thought I'd try being a hero, at least to one person." Her smile was almost bashful.

Batch had to look away from it before her heart beat out of her chest.

"Carillo has that effect," she murmured. She went light-headed when Hooper's smile grew wide.

"Oh, it wasn't for him, Batch. Although he does his best, as my father might say."

"You talk a lot of nonsense." Hogwash, that's what Ruby had called it. Batch crossed her arms to hide her shaking hands. "I don't know what it means. But I don't need... any of that."

Hooper's smile fell. She pulled away from the door but didn't come any closer. "I can go," she offered, voice low and still gentle. She rubbed the back of her neck. "I shouldn't have pushed. I knew that. It's just that I was surprised, you know."

Batch didn't know a damn thing, except she'd gotten Hooper here and nobody had pushed her to do it. She shook her head and Hooper's smile returned. "Stay," Batch said anyway, although it was about the only thing she knew to ask for.

"You're pretty brave, aren't you, Batch?" Hooper's voice was no longer so soft or smooth. She glanced away when Batch opened her mouth to argue, but then looked back, the heat of the midday sun in her eyes. "I mean it."

Batch bit back a denial and held her breath until the high, strained laugh in her throat died. She finally shook her head again. There wasn't anything to say to something like that, false but sweet. She looked down and kept her gaze there even after hearing the scuff of Hooper's boots on the floor and then seeing them in front of her.

"The first time I saw you... I'd already gotten tangled up with Brannan's people on the road, and in town I met Carillo and John and the others. But I wasn't about to get into a situation not of my own making."

"That's because you're wiser than me," Batch pointed out without lifting her head.

"Shush," Hooper told her, with just a hint of temper. "I am telling you that I felt that way until I saw you. You were... barely able to stand, and yet you were ready to pull your gun when I approached the jail, because you thought I was a threat to the people you cared about, and I realized…"

"That I had the shakes?" Batch filled in when Hooper didn't go on. She put her hands to her cheeks, felt them burn with a lifetime's worth of shame.

"That you were going to stand guard even if it killed you. And now you…"

"What?" Batch jerked her head up and let her hands fall, baring her blush to the light of the oil lamp and Hooper's bright eyes. "Am scared silly to think I might kiss a girl?"

Hooper's expression did things Batch didn't have the words to describe. Ruby might have, but Batch was only glad Ruby wasn't here to see it.

"Might?" Hooper echoed, then made a sound. Her voice was hard to describe too, rough, but also pleased, or a word for the kind of pleased that made Batch's already warm cheeks sting. "You will." She stared at Batch for another moment, like she was caught up and couldn't stop, and then said in an entirely different voice, "You face things. That's what I meant. Maybe you didn't before." She silenced Batch's objection before Batch could make it. "But you do now. Maybe even too much. Yeah, you're quaking in your boots to have me here, but you have me here all the same. You're brave."

Batch didn't even lift her chin to argue about any quaking. Possibly because even she could hear the fear in her answer. "You don't know any of that."

Hooper shrugged but kept her gaze steady. "Got a feeling."

Batch scoffed despite the worrying flips in her stomach.

Hooper shrugged again. "I told you, that's how it is, with my… in my family. We get feelings. And I've seen you in action. I'm seeing you now."

She wasn't seeing anything. If they were in a cathouse, Hooper wouldn't even be getting her money's worth.

"I still have my gun belt on," Batch said with a frown, and wished she could get mad enough to stop worrying when Hooper's face lit up.

"Then take it off," Hooper answered, slow and husky, reaching for the buckle herself when Batch was frozen. Batch only remembered to move at the clank of metal, and reached down to finish untying the holster from her thigh. Hooper caught the belt easily, without looking away, and rolled it up loosely before setting it down on the table behind Batch. The action brought her a mite closer.

Batch thought about saying she was still in her coat, but wasn't sure what she would do if Hooper took that as well. She pulled her work knife from her belt on her own and tossed that with everything else.

They were face to face. Hooper was holding herself still, but barely, rocking on her heels a little, face flushed, lips parted.

"Just touch me already." Batch meant it for a snap, for a growl, but it was as soft as everything else between them so far. She was quaking in her boots, and gave up waiting to put a hand on Hooper's arm.

Hooper blinked. For all of a heartbeat, she stared at Batch as though she'd never had any intention of touching her. She lifted her hands as if she wanted to rest them on the sides of Batch's face, but in the end, it was just her mouth, soft, against Batch's mouth. One kiss, and then another, although the second was the trailing, lingering kind that Batch didn't know how to respond to except to curl her fingers into Hooper's lapels.

She ought to feel shock, but it was warmth that spread through her chest and down to her guts and up to her hands and all through her blood. Hooper was humming tension beneath her touch, like Batch had put a hand to the back of a guitar. She kissed Batch again despite whatever was making her tremble, finally sliding her palm against Batch's cheek, then the side of her neck. Her palm was smoother than it ought to be, and she was gentle, but Batch wasn't protesting.

The table dug into the small of her back. That hardly bothered Batch either. Hooper was stealing her breath and Batch couldn't seem to care. Not even when the kissing ended, then renewed elsewhere, Hooper's mouth hot at the hollow of Batch's throat while she slipped her hands down to Batch's waist.

"You don't have to, you know," Hooper reminded her, breath damp and warm where it crept beneath Batch's shirt and the top few buttons Batch had left open.

Batch had nothing to glower at but the walls and the top of Hooper's head. "When I can't take it…"

"You'll let me know?" Hooper finished, pleased in that hot, stinging way again. It could have been a dare, the kind of thing said to make Batch lose her temper and keep going, but quitting was the last thing on her mind. Anyway, Hooper was pleased, her special pleased, and kissed her way back up to Batch's mouth while she undid the belt to Batch's pants as smoothly as she'd unhitched Batch's gun.

Batch turned her head to suck in a breath, and flung her other hand somewhere behind her until she found the edge of the table and held it tight. "Your fingers," she whined and couldn't cringe for it, not with her legs already shaking. She hadn't thought it would feel as good, but Hooper wriggled her hand into her pants and barely touched her, and Batch's cunny throbbed and began to grow wet.

Hooper dropped her face to the side of Batch's neck and dragged in a long, heavy breath. "Oh."

For a moment, two, when she slid her other hand to the back of Batch's thigh, Batch imagined Hooper might lift her up onto the little table and step between her legs to take her, with her fingers at least. A mad thought, since Hooper couldn't lift her and the table wouldn't support her. But she gasped out something, maybe a warning, and Hooper held still and breathed hard against her neck before just touching her again.

"Months," Hooper complained, rough and indignant, leaving panting, shivery kisses beneath Batch's ear and stroking her cat without daring to dip her fingers inside. She pulled in another breath. "Scent of roses and now the rest of you too. I can't...."

Hooper spoke a lot of nonsense, and she was a liar, because she could and she did, finally pressing her palm where Batch needed it and not even shushing Batch again when her gasps carried to the ceiling.

Batch came apart with her eyes closed and one hand slapped over her mouth, too late to muffle most of her cries. That was the first time. When she kept trembling and her legs were too weak to hold her, Hooper wrapped an arm around her waist and tugged her close. Batch breathed in pomade and sweat and hid her face in Hooper's coat when Hooper started to pet her again, like all she'd come up here for was to make Batch slick and hot for her.

Batch was quieter the second time, hiccupping into Hooper's shoulder and pressing so close it should've been an embarrassment. She was supposed to be getting some sugar, giving Hooper some too, not pleading and holding tighter when Hooper pulled her hand from her pants to let Batch catch her breath.

"Oh," Hooper said again, surprised, though she must have done this before.

Batch opened her eyes, then turned her head to look up.

Hooper looked back, eyes big and bright as moons, her lips bitten and red. Batch's hand moved without her say-so, curving itself to the side of Hooper's face and tipping it down to meet Batch as she came up.

Batch was wild and a fool, clear-eyed and sober. She couldn't manage sweet or soft, but at least the kiss was slow. She sank her fingers into shining, pomaded hair, so short it slipped from her hold and she had to try it again. Hooper made a little noise, liking that, and it was an easy pleasure to give, carding and combing Hooper's hair while Hooper took her clumsy kiss. Batch finally pulled away only when she didn't know what else to do except try to return the favor.

Their faces were close, their mouths open as they breathed hard. Hooper made that noise again, and since Batch hadn't removed her hand, she ran it once more through Hooper's hair. The barber had nearly shaved it at the bottom, above the nape, and when she scratched there, Hooper ducked her head to mutter against Batch's throat.

Batch was damp all down between her legs and still shaking, but Hooper's breath there, in the hollow of her throat where Hooper had kissed her before, made her ache in a way she barely recognized.

"There's a bed," she reminded Hooper, but it was as far as she got. Hooper put her hands on Batch's shoulders, and it was not graceful, the way they tumbled down onto the bed. Hooper still had her gun belt strapped on. They were both dressed. The bed was no larger for having two people in it and they were at the wrong angle as well.

Batch landed on top of Hooper with Hooper's arms curled around her hips to soften the fall. The position was uncomfortable for only a few quick beats of her heart, and then Hooper wriggled back and spread her legs and suddenly there was some room for Batch between them.

Batch wanted to laugh and didn't know why. It wasn't a mean feeling. More of a funny one, a thought that also made her want to laugh. Hooper had her arms around Batch but let them fall to the bed when Batch slid over her, and she didn't say a word when Batch rose up on her knees. She just watched her, wide-eyed and pretty and armed to the teeth.

Batch did laugh, high and giddy before she stopped it. She leaned back down quickly to press her mouth to Hooper's neck, and to her ear, somewhat startled from her dizzy pleasure to find the other ear also had scarring at the top. But then Hooper sighed her name, and Batch went back to kissing her skin, untying Hooper's kerchief impatiently when it got in her way.

Hooper laughed at that. Batch rose up again, intending to remark on that, only Hooper's clothing had all these buttons. Men's clothing did, all down the front, but it was different with valleys and curves behind them and Hooper breathing hard and watching her.

Batch shakily tried a few buttons; even sober, her hands were unreliable things when she was anticipating warm skin. The vest was slow work, the shirt beneath it slightly faster. She pulled that open only to find a thin chemise slip tucked into Hooper's pants that Hooper's breasts were straining against. She was more blessed there than Batch was; the slip hardly seemed like anything, plump swells and dark nipples more than visible.

Batch stopped, then swallowed. She thought faintly that she understood now what Hooper had meant when she'd said she was surprised. Batch had expected to feel something during all this, had admired Hooper and thought her pretty. She had not expected to look down on her like this and feel desire heavy and wet all through her insides and down between her thighs. She wondered if Hooper felt that, looking at her.

She swallowed again, dry and painful, before pulling up the slip to run her palms over bare skin, only to freeze again when she didn't know where to touch first.

Hooper put a hand over hers. "Batch?"

"It's like I'm starving, I want so much." Batch forced her eyes up to meet Hooper's. Hooper had no right to look so happy but Batch didn't stop her. "But all I can think to do is touch you. Is that..." She didn't know how to finish the question, except, "What do you want?"

"I'm normally better than this," Hooper answered, admitted almost, then shifted a bit to try to sit up. "Help me?" She gestured to her gun and her belt, and that, Batch could assist her with, and did, turning away to lower Hooper's weapon to the ground. When she turned back, Hooper was working on her coat, so Batch recalled hers and shrugged that off too. It meant she could move more freely, Hooper as well. In no time at all, they were turned the right way on the bed and Batch was on her back with a pillow beneath her head and Hooper bare-chested and settling over her.

Batch had a passing thought that they should've taken the time to remove their boots so their pants might follow, but Hooper was flushed all down her body and silently begging for Batch to put her hands on her, and that was a more urgent concern. Hooper hadn't finished even once, so Batch tried not to be too distracted by the weight of Hooper's breasts in her hands or the way Hooper watched her explore them. When she realized Hooper was trembling with want, she dipped her hand down, and Hooper guided it where she wanted it and held it there, riding it instead of letting Batch try to please her. Hooper closed her eyes and made quiet sounds, but with her head thrown back and that flush growing darker down her chest. Batch was left to burn brightly and feel both covetous and proud when Hooper finally fell against her to catch her breath.

She was warm and sweet, and the crush of her breasts against Batch was nice. So nice, Batch nearly asked her to move so she wouldn't want more. But she did want more, scaring her even through the haze of pleasure. It was Tinney's fault, somehow, for making her think of things beyond the day to day, to wonder about futures.

Though she didn't know what Tinney would make of the two of them tangled up like this.

She reached up, careful, to smooth Hooper's hair, and Hooper hummed and allowed it.

Batch ached, and the rapid pounding of her heart might just kill her, but her blood was singing. She was wet, or still wet, and wanted to pin Hooper down to look at her again and touch her all over. Hooper had no reason to let her do that, of course. Hooper had no reason not to get up and leave right that second.

"Want a smoke?" Batch offered, knowing she had to say something. Anyway, even after everything, the cigarette Hooper had rolled for her was dangling, if probably crushed, from the chunk of her hair that had fallen free. She plucked it out and curled the loose hair behind her ear before leaning over to light her smoke with the lamp, the action forcing Hooper to sit up. Batch inhaled once before passing it over.

Hooper considered it before she took it, then said, "I generally only smoke when I'm nervous," before handing it back.

Batch smoked mostly for something to do with her hands, to pass the time. Tinney was right; she did need to find herself an interest.

She looked up, still catching her breath, only to lose it again at the sight of Hooper bare from the waist up, bold as anything, and fussing her with hair.

Batch stubbed the cigarette against the metal base of the lamp, then again on the already stained and scratched surface of the table.

Hooper was trying to arrange her hair to what it had been, but sighed and dropped her hands when she saw Batch watching.

Batch's grin slipped out before she could help it. "Missing your hair concoction already?"

Hooper lifted her eyebrows as if offended, but then snorted and said, "Yes," before adding, "but I don't mind how it got this way." Her smile was wicked and almost enough to set Batch to blushing.

Hoping that would go unnoticed, Batch focused on other things, or tried to. "When you're nervous?" she remembered aloud. That didn't seem right, and had to be more of Hooper's nonsense.

Hooper merely shrugged, which drew Batch's gaze down to her breasts again. Hooper's smile widened, but she shifted backward and turned slightly to start pulling at her bootlaces. Batch should have asked if she planned to stay longer, since removing her boots implied that, but in truth, watching Hooper make quick work of the laces was mesmerizing.

Hooper's boots had just plopped to the floor when she turned to straddle Batch's lap, putting her breasts nearly in Batch's face before she settled. Despite that, Batch's attention went to her face, confused until Hooper went to work on Batch's clothing with the same speed and cleverness she'd used on her boot laces. Batch's vest was unbuttoned and parted within moments, although Hooper paused, waiting for Batch's hasty nod before she did the same to Batch's shirt.

Then Hooper made a noise, the pleased sound she'd made before.

Batch glanced down at herself, knowing she'd see a small, loosely tied short corset and the faded slip beneath that. Both were old. The corset wasn't even the type Ruby or Eulalia wore, years out of fashion, although Batch couldn't wear a longer corset unless she was in skirts, which she obviously wasn't. The short corset and her slip were both plain white, or had been, with some stains appearing over time, along with Batch's needlework where patches had been needed.

Batch had a job now. She could afford some new things. But buying them in this town was a struggle if you were Batch. People would tease or outright laugh.

She nearly tugged her shirt closed under Hooper's heavy stare.

"I…" She hesitated. "I know it's hardly a dress. But I always liked this part, at least, and no one could see." Except whoever was in her bed at that moment, and usually they had no comment one way or the other. "I did have nicer clothes for a while, when I was working. Finer, though no softer."

"Stockings and drawers too? Lace and all?" Hooper surprised her with the question. She was bright-eyed again, breathless. "I'll bet you were a sight."

Batch stared back at her for several breathless moments of her own before remembering to blink. "With a ribbon 'round my neck," she added and tapped the side of her throat. "The bow tied just so."

The sound Hooper made this time was more of a whine. She touched Batch's collarbone, then her neck in that same spot in a touch so light Batch shivered. When she tugged at the kerchief Batch still wore, and undid the knot to pull it free, Batch didn't say a word.

Hooper touched Batch's hair next, the strands that had fallen loose from where Batch had tucked them behind her ear. "Do you ever dress like that now?"

Goosebumps followed Hooper's gentle touches. Batch shuddered and turned her head, but allowed Hooper to tug more of her hair free. Some of it was still damp and even more strongly scented of soap and roses.

Batch shook her head. "I don't really know... any of that. Not like a real lady, or even someone like Ruby. It'd be a joke. Batch in a dress..." She trailed off, then considered, and reconsidered, Hooper's chest. "Do you?"

"Hell no." Hooper snorted again, continuing to play with Batch's hair. "You'll never catch me in a skirt." She paused to grin. "Unless it's with my hands up yours."

Batch made the pleased sound this time, thinking of all her borrowed flash and her red drawers and Hooper looking at Batch like she was now before lifting Batch's skirts to do as she pleased. Batch would have let Hooper touch her for free, might even have kept here there throughout the early mornings, with the curtains drawn, and sat with her during meals.

Hooper was motionless and calm except for her eyes, which could have been those of a hungry animal in the dark before she put her hands on either side of Batch's ribs and slowly leaned down.

"Batch," she asked after a while, barely lifting her lips from her work of kissing the top of Batch's small breasts where the corset pushed them out. "What's your name? Your real name, I mean. Tinney says you didn't choose to be Batch."

Batch blinked her eyes open, and frowned vaguely as she tried to remember. Her name. Her real one. Her thoughts were slow.

Hooper didn't seem to mind that Batch didn't answer. She hummed and said, "You're lovely, Batch or whoever you are." She sat back up with a sigh. "So lovely you don't know what it does to me."

She trailed a touch up Batch's thigh. Batch regretted the clothes she still had on, but wasn't going to move now except to toss her head.

"You don't need to romance me." Batch never could shut up when she should. At least Hooper didn't seem offended. She just scoffed and dropped down to kiss Batch's breasts again. Batch slid a hand into

Hooper's hair, petting, since they both liked it and Hooper's hairstyle was already done for. "Some do that, buy the girls things, combs and ribbons and candy, like they're sweethearts." Though some had been, or maybe that was how one got a sweetheart, even in a cathouse.

"Did you like getting them?" Hooper returned her attentions to Batch's neck. Batch tipped her head to allow it.

"Nobody gave me anything." Surely that was obvious. "Although once a girl, a friend, offered me her earrings, and to put them on me."

Hooper sat up, then gave Batch a look so knowing it made Batch hot down to her toes. Hooper was gentle, however, when she touched Batch's earlobe. "And did you wear them?"

Batch gave a small shake of her head. "That would have been another joke." She waved quickly at herself, a rawboned, skinny drunk. "Wouldn't know what to do with nice things. I'd look silly done up like one of them, proper lady or not."

Hooper held her gaze for a long time, long enough for Batch to open and shut her mouth a few times without thinking of what she should say. Then Hooper held Batch's chin and kissed her, soft, before resuming all her kisses to the rest of Batch's bared skin. "I could get you earrings."

Batch's scoff was weak. "You should be saving up to buy a homestead or... whatever it is you plan to do. When you go."

"Oh..." Hooper drew out the word, "when I have seen enough of the rest of the world, I'll go home." Her kisses were harder now, but not hurtful. They made Batch want to wriggle and ask for Hooper's hands on her corset laces. She was beside herself at the thought. Hooper kept caressing her without seeming to notice Batch's restless shivering. "People can always use help out there. There's always something that needs doing. Maybe I'll build a home." She kissed between Batch's breasts, then her voice grew even more husky. "Get me a wife."

A jolt went through Batch. "You can't—"

"Funny town, where I'm from." Hooper lightly scraped her teeth over soft flesh. "That kind of thing don't matter much."

She had to be lying. She must be.

Batch pulled her hand from Hooper's hair and swallowed her gasps. "You do like a tall tale, don't you? Everyone knows I don't need to be wooed. A few months ago, a drink would have done it." She stared at Hooper defiantly when Hooper raised her head. "What? You know it's true. Not all of us tell pretty stories, Hooper. Not all of us even have pretty stories."

"My given name is Olivia," Hooper said in return. "I told you that once, you and me and Tinney, and you said it back to me. It'd make me happy to hear you say it now, with my mouth on you."

"Didn't you hear?" Batch's chest was so tight that the beat of her heart should have been painful. "Didn't you hear what I said?"

"Oh, I hear everything," Hooper assured her, not a trace of a smile on her face or in her voice, completely serious despite her silly boasting. "Long before I ever met you, I heard about you. But I think you saying my name is one of the sweeter sounds on this earth, and I have spent many a night wondering how it would feel if you called it out while we shared a bed."

"My landlady might hear," Batch said. It was the first thing that came to mind that was fit to say aloud and also completely untrue.

"Then call it quietly," Hooper argued, some of her smile returning to her voice at last.

"Olivia," Batch tried, a croak. Hardly worth dreaming about.

Hooper stopped, and closed her eyes, and let out a ragged breath. "Batch," she complained.

"Olivia," Batch said again, gentler, hot again all through her body at just one word. Hooper had not imagined her saying it. That could not be. But Batch said it again, curling her fingers down one scarred ear and then into Hooper's short hair. It was a nice name, worth repeating softly in a shared bed, even if that bed was lumpy and small.

Hooper seemed to agree. She begged Batch for it three more times before she unlaced her and unclothed her. And though she didn't ask again, her mouth otherwise occupied, Batch gave it to her anyway, then, and then once more with her fingers slippery and Hooper trembling.

She might have said it again as they were falling asleep, Hooper curved along her back and playing with her hair. But, if she did, it wasn't more than a whisper, a dream to make Batch blush when she woke in the light of midmorning.

Three

HOOPER was gone by then, as she had said she would be. She had people to take up to the geysers. She might stay up there with them for a while before heading back, or she might be going on north or east, or all the way down to Los Cerros without stopping. Batch hadn't asked. It didn't matter. It shouldn't matter. Batch had had lovers before, for work or pleasure or whatever reason. Most only a night or two anyway, so the whereabouts and plans of Olivia Hooper were nothing to her except maybe the interest of a friend. If they were friends.

Batch wasn't sure they were even that. All the talk of earrings and hometowns and names was just talk. Even Batch knew people said ridiculous things in bed.

She cleaned up and got dressed before heading out to make sure Carillo had gotten some rest, and then she took a shift walking the streets and keeping an eye out for trouble that hopefully wouldn't come. That night, she spent her money on another bath, flushing hot despite the lukewarm water when she found herself lost in dreams over soap bubbles.

She ate supper at a table, with Tinney, and let him talk about some scandal back East that had been in all the papers without understanding a thing about financial dealings—although she accepted his opinion of all the dealers. He let her have his stack of old newspapers when he was done, and she spent part of her night squinting at the articles and searching for something to interest her. Something for the future. But reading gave her a headache and she didn't know too many of the words, and all the advertised jobs in Los Cerros involved typing machines and other mysteries.

In her room again, late at night, looking into the mirror, she considered the white kerchief with blue specks that had been left behind, folded neatly on her dresser. She hadn't worn it, of course; Ruby might have recognized it. But alone, Batch rolled it up and tied it, just so, imagining it was a ribbon, imagining that it was a gift and not something forgotten.

She woke early, and shooed Carillo out of the jail to finish his shift for him there, waking and releasing the two farmhands who were the worse for wear with drink, and washing out the pot of coffee that must have been on the stove since yesterday. She didn't need to be there, she couldn't help but think. The immediate danger had passed, and whatever else the landowner and business types might try, it would likely be through the courts or the banks as Tinney said.

The future was coming sooner than she'd expected.

She supposed she could help around on someone else's homestead. She did have the skills for that. Maybe she could find a widow who'd feel more comfortable with Batch around than a bunch of rowdy workers. Batch could do the hard work, digging and such, or even a little cooking and house chores. She'd done all of that as a child after her mother had passed. She could ask Tinney to put the word out for her. She might even get someone to help her improve her skills with the needle. It would be nice to be able to sew her own underthings with small, neat stitches, and possibly add ribbon or a flounce where no one could see.

It wasn't a terrible idea, even if it also made Batch sigh and pace restlessly up and down the street. It seemed a safe future, a good one, for someone like her. After all, she wasn't going to have a place of her own. She'd never manage that with her pay.

Perhaps it was that thinking of it made her realize how sweet the notion was. Not just a flounce or two, but a place. Though what she would do there, she couldn't imagine. Live off a garden and a cow and some chickens. Add a room for Tinney, if he needed one. Sleep in a bed in a room with papered walls. Roll over to see...

She stopped herself there, and walked some more until she found Carillo outside the bakery eating his lunch. Batch bought a roll leftover from the day before and joined him, although Carillo greeted those passing by and she looked far too often down to the end of the street, where any wagons returning from up north might be seen.

"There really isn't much to do." Batch didn't mean to say it, but she had eaten her roll too quickly.

Carillo, sipping from a cup filled with coffee, stopped to look at her. Then he lowered the cup, waiting.

Batch made a face, then exhaled before putting her shoulders back. "I mean, what are your plans? Now that things are settling, they'll make you sheriff for real."

Carillo's eyebrows flew up. "No, they won't," he disagreed, his surprise obvious. "There will be no place for someone like me when this place decides it will be civilized." Batch frowned and Carillo shook his head. "Brannan acted greedily. If he'd just waited, he could have joined the other rich men buying up the area and leaving the rest to farmers too tired to protest. The rich men and the big farmers needed me. But they won't once the state law starts being enforced here. They'll want someone around who is afraid of them, obeys them. That's not me."

"You saved their necks," Batch protested foolishly.

Carillo smiled a little and offered her some of his coffee, which was cold.

"They'll want a sheriff who goes to their churches and socials and evicts people like Tinney, or who keeps people like you and Ruby to the edge of town. That's their way and you know it as well as I do."

She hadn't. Or at least, she hadn't wanted to see it. Whiskey dulled the vision and removed good sense. Batch was unfortunately clearheaded now. She faced things.

"What will you do?" she asked at last, handing Carillo his cup and then watching him finish everything but the dregs, which he tossed to the side.

"There's more to see than this place," he answered. But it took him a while, and he shrugged as he said it. "Don't worry about it now, Batch."

Since that was all she would do, Batch walked off, avoiding the hotel and anywhere else she might have been tempted to forget it all in a drink. She played dominoes with Tinney, and let him read some kind of poetry at her for a while, thinking mostly that Hooper would probably like verse all flowery and grand about fairies and far-off places.

After, she went to the hotel to fetch Tin some food, and some for herself as well. And when Tinney had eaten and sent her off, insisting she was young and would find something better to do than hide indoors with him, she returned to the hotel to bring them their plates and cutlery.

It was only then, with the downstairs space full of people who seemed grateful to be away from the health resort and in a place with good food and drink in abundance, that she spotted the tall figure seated across from Ruby at Ruby's usual table.

They had their heads together, like kids telling secrets, making Batch wonder once again what those two had discussed all those months ago to make them such fast friends. They might have grown close simply for being women who would not be warmly welcomed by any of the ladies at the tables currently occupied by spa guests. Even though, from her manners, Ruby had once been one of those ladies. A few of the spa guests did glance over while Batch watched, frowning in disapproval or confusion or something else at either Ruby for drinking and playing cards, or Hooper for her pants and how she stretched out her long legs to take up space.

It was just possible some of those proper ladies enjoyed the sight, even if they'd likely never say so. All the same, Batch imagined them trying to sweet-talk Hooper on the journeys to and from the spa and took herself off to the bath room before Bill could come over and ask her about her scowl.

Once there, she decided against the cost of another full bath and just washed from a basin, splashing water on her face and the back of her neck, and scrubbing her hands.

Those ladies downstairs looked like they hadn't seen dirt a day in their lives. Hooper might prefer that.

An absolutely fool notion that bothered Batch despite how she had no reason for it to bother her. Hooper might find different girls all the time. She hadn't done anything to say otherwise, and everyone knew Batch wasn't special.

It might have felt that way, for a moment or two, in the dark and quiet, with Hooper curled around her and nuzzling behind her ear, but that was probably more Batch's confusion at the entire situation than any wrongdoing or hints on Hooper's part. Carillo had been kind to Batch once in her younger years and earned her instant devotion from then on. Batch was like that. It wasn't anybody's fault but her own.

With that thought fixed in her mind, she combed her hair out and pinned it back up before leaving. She hadn't yet decided whether to greet Ruby and Hooper or to try to slip out through the kitchen, but when she stopped by the stairs to sneak a peek at the main room, Hooper turned toward her as if aware of exactly where Batch was and had been.

No one snuck up on her, Hooper had said. Maybe at least one of Hooper's tall tales wasn't entirely untrue.

Batch tugged at the attached collar of her shirt, realized she'd left her kerchief with Tinney, and came forward as all part of one anxious motion. She should have buttoned her shirt all the way. She should have worn a sturdier vest. Hooper's gaze was on her bare throat and Batch was not good or decent or proper but she was blushing like a parson's daughter by the time she reached the table.

"Batch!" Ruby called out gaily; perhaps she had thrown back a few before Batch had arrived, which was unlike her but she might have been feeling merry.

Batch gave her a smile she suspected was twitchy. Then her gaze went right back to Hooper for as long as she could hold it, which wasn't very long at all, since the way Hooper was looking at her put her in mind of whispers, and Hooper waking her up to kiss her goodbye, and Hooper making a sound near to a growl when she'd finally, truly had to go. Though Batch had likely dreamed that part, or even all of it.

Hooper jumped up from her seat and bobbed her head in a greeting, then reached for her hat before seeming to realize she'd left it on the table. She smiled with barely a pause. "Miss Batch."

Batch lost her breath and stood there, lips parted, staring in befuddled amazement at Hooper until Ruby delicately cleared her throat. Then Batch got her mouth shut at least. She put a shaking hand to her face and sat down without paying much attention to where, only thinking she had better sit soon, before Hooper could pull out her chair for her.

An embarrassing, incredible possibility.

Miss Batch. No one called Batch Miss. Not even Tinney. Hooper hadn't done it either, not until now.

Of course, now Hooper had seen Batch's underthings, and heard her long for prettier ones and the knowledge to wear them like Ruby did.

It might have been a joke, a cruel one, but Batch realized she wasn't bristling or even walking out. She was doubtlessly red in the face and she had a lump in her throat, but she wasn't angry.

Possibly, a voice in her mind whispered, because Hooper had said it. Hooper, who wanted a wife. A wife. If anyone was going to say such things and mean them, it would be her.

Too late to hide how flustered she was—and she was, nearly squirming under Hooper's warm regard—Batch turned toward Ruby.

Ruby took some time examining the locket around her neck as though she'd never seen it before.

Her hand still on her cheek, Batch glanced to Hooper again. "Evening," she greeted them both, although her voice was soft and she had to quickly look away.

"Evening!" Ruby returned, locket forgotten. "So nice to see you out and about again, Batch. I know it must be hard, but you have been missed."

Ruby hadn't known Batch as anything but sober, except for possibly a few days before then, and so couldn't have missed the old version of her, but Batch kindly didn't say so. She couldn't say much of anything still, with her heart in her throat and Miss ringing in her ears. Batch was a ridiculous person. A soak. A romping gal-boy with no manners. She wasn't a Mister and she sure as hell was not a Miss to anyone. Miss was what they called a lady in a house or a schoolteacher. Miss or Ma'am, to show respect.

She'd never called Hooper that. Neither had Carillo, or Ruby for that matter.

Batch pulled her hand from her face and did her best to make her voice normal. "Miss Hooper."

Hooper nearly flinched, then recovered enough to give Batch a little grin. "Just Hooper will do."

Batch nodded eagerly. "Hooper," she agreed.

"Thank you, Miss Batch." Hooper gave her another grin, far too pleased with herself when Batch was struck dumb again. "I knew you'd understand."

Ruby hummed. The sound would've meant nothing if Batch didn't know her as well as she did. "Hooper here says more and more people are asking to stop in our little hamlet. I can't tell if that speaks to the quality of this establishment or the strict conditions to achieve better health up at the hot springs."

Hooper turned toward Ruby, her eyes almost sparkling. "A bit of both, I suspect. Although I don't know how much longer the resort is going to insist on the treatments up there with how so many people complain. Still not sure what all exactly it's supposed to be healing."

"I'm certain it does wonders," Ruby remarked, but with a smile that said she didn't mean it. Hooper smiled back and gestured to the deck of cards between them. Ruby turned a card over, and so did Hooper, and then they started bickering over rules. Whatever they were playing looked like a child's game. They certainly weren't playing for money.

Batch supposed Ruby didn't get to be silly much. Maybe that was what she and Hooper liked about each other. Batch just liked watching them. It gave her time to calm her heart and hopefully return to a shade other than red, and they were sweet, arguing over points instead of money. Ruby hadn't been happy when she'd first arrived here. Not that Batch could remember, anyway. Oh, she'd smiled, charming, teasing smiles at Carillo that had set Batch to frowning for a while, but she hadn't been like this. Some of that was his doing, and some of that was likely because of John, and Eulalia, and even this moment with Hooper.

Hooper was radiant for their mock-argument, but she was leaning back with one elbow on the table, and her lips were soft and they curved up often in amusement, even when she finally lost the debate.

Batch knew she was staring and only yanked her gaze away when Ruby turned to her, one eyebrow arched.

"You need anything, honey? Some beer?"

"Or I could get you tea," Hooper offered, bringing another moment of silence to the table. Hooper scratched her nose. "I noticed you didn't drink that beer the other night," she added in explanation. Her eyes were still bright and her cheeks were dark. It would be a pleasure for her to do it, her clear gaze told Batch.

Batch pulled in a breath then turned, strangely terrified, to Ruby.

Ruby glanced between them, her expression as blank as she could make it, which was a lot, as she was a woman who played cards for a living. But she finally tilted her head toward Hooper and announced in a crisp yet calm voice, "A cup of tea would be lovely, Hooper."

Hooper hopped up and headed to the bar as if that had been an order. Ruby kept her eyes on Batch.

"I can drink tea," Batch insisted after a while, wiping her palms on her knees. She did like tea, but people tended to give her coffee. She liked that too, and it was a lot less fuss, so she didn't mind.

Ruby nodded once, slowly. "I'll pour the first time."

Batch frowned, then recalled the tea service Eulalia was most proud of, then blanched. Hooper fell back into her seat before Batch could think of what to say, and the proud look on her face was going to set Batch on fire. She couldn't explain it, but that was how it felt.

Hooper and Ruby went back to their cards, although Ruby first said pointedly, "Thank you, Hooper," so Batch did the same, and wondered distantly if Hooper also felt like she was quietly burning from the inside out. Batch wanted to get her something for it in return, but Hooper had a drink already, even if she wasn't drinking it, and everything else that came to mind did not seem soothing.

Batch pulled at her collar and nearly jumped out of her skin when John arrived with a tray.

"Ladies." John seemed amused, but he smiled kindly at Batch, so Batch said nothing except a thanks. Her attention was on the tea things anyway. It wasn't quite the full set, not like it would be for real ladies, but on the tray was a pot, a bowl of sugar with tiny silver tongs, a pitcher of milk or cream, a slightly dry lemon cut into a few wedges on a plate, and two cups with saucers, all of it delicate white china decorated with blue flowers. Not Eulalia's best set, thank goodness; Batch would've been too scared to touch that. It was bad enough to see this set here, fine and breakable, next to two sturdy whiskey glasses.

Tea at a poker table. Practically unheard of. Nonetheless, if anyone nearby had anything to say about it, they kept it to themselves or said it very quietly.

Batch watched intently as Ruby poured and asked Batch how she took her tea. Ruby lifted the saucers with the cups, even though it would have been easier to leave them on the table or just use the saucer instead of the cup to cool the drink down faster, like folks did with their coffee when in a hurry.

Batch got milk and sugar in hers and held it—the saucer too—without drinking it, while the other two went back to their friendly bickering. She thought maybe they were doing it on purpose now, an act to give Batch time or to ignore how sometimes her saucer and cup rattled. Batch did bristle at that, but shouting at them would've taken their smiles away, and she did want something to sip while they pulled cards and threw them down and gleefully insulted each other.

When they started to play for real, Batch ought to go. But they weren't yet, so she stayed, and watched them, and finally, had some of her tea. The steam stung her cheeks. So did Hooper's many glances.

Olivia Hooper had no call to look so pleased. Batch didn't fault her for it, though she didn't understand it. Batch had to sit straighter to hold the cup level, unless she wanted to slouch down and leave it on her belly, which Ruby would not approve of, from anyone. So Batch sat straight, and sipped tea while watching Hooper until she realized she was watching Hooper, and then she'd watch Ruby for a few minutes before her gaze would drift back to Hooper's eyes and her hair and her chin and the scar on her ear.

The room started to get loud as more came in for food or a good time. Hooper and Ruby switched to poker, although not yet playing for money, and asked Batch if she wanted to join and didn't seem to mind that she didn't. She should. She knew that. But she didn't actually like the game and she wasn't good at it, and it was nice, listening to them and laughing once or twice when Hooper would look put out or make a big deal of pulling a card out of her sleeve like the clumsiest cheat ever.

Batch poured herself another cup, adding lemon this time, the saucer rattling away, then put her tea down to go return the tray and the rest of the service to the kitchen. She was glad she did, because when she returned there were two others seated at the table, and the card playing had grown more serious. A tea service wouldn't have belonged.

Batch shouldn't be there if she didn't intend to play, but though one of the other players, in a city suit, frowned in her direction when she sat back down, the other, a sheepherder with a few acres of fruit trees from deeper in the valley, nodded to her, and since he didn't raise a fuss, perhaps the other fellow didn't feel it was worth it.

Batch couldn't tell if the stranger was a good player or not. The sheepherder, whose name she thought was Bianchini but couldn't be sure, wasn't, but the stakes weren't high yet or maybe he thought he was good, so he kept playing. The stranger could have been an excellent player and Batch wouldn't have noticed, too distracted by how still Hooper could be when it mattered, and noticing the difference between her practiced smiles and her real ones.

Carillo came in briefly to look around but didn't stop by. He merely exchanged a questioning look with Batch and a longer, more intimate one with Ruby that had set Batch to staring at Hooper again until Hooper had looked up. Hooper could remind Batch of kisses, to her mouth and elsewhere, with just a glance, and Batch dropped her eyes to keep her blush from worsening.

Batch had never chosen a lover before. At least, not like this. She would've asked herself why now and why Hooper, but Hooper had offered it, hadn't she? And Hooper had Tinney's affection, and Carillo's admiration, and Ruby's friendship, and she was sweet despite how she teased, and, well, Batch liked the look of her. She had at first and now she did more and more, making her insides as hot and bubbling as one of the springs.

It was ridiculous.

Batch didn't mind it, not one bit, except for the small quiver of fear that shot through her when she caught herself staring in front of so many others, and the way her hands shook when she imagined how she must seem to everyone else, flushed and barely able to hold a cup and saucer.

Bianchini, if that was his name, caught her eye and gestured to her cup with a friendly, sotted smile. "Never seen you with that, like one of the teetotalers up at the springs."

"I can get you some," Batch offered, although he seemed content with whatever he had been drinking. Whiskey, from the smell of it, but the kind John sold and not the kind from the camps or from the crowded, cheaper parts of larger towns. "Bianchini, right?"

He slapped her on the shoulder after trying to take her hand despite the tea. "Lorenzo, please, Blue. Lorenzo."

The tea sloshed about in the cup, pale from too much milk. Batch considered it another moment, then set both cup and saucer carefully onto the table so the rattling wouldn't disturb the game.

She needn't have bothered. The table had gone quiet.

"No one ever did explain Blue to me." Hooper spoke first, gentle and not, glaring at Bianchini then turning a softer look on Batch when Batch raised her head.

"Or to me," Ruby added. "Mariano won't."

"It's a joke." Batch took a deep breath that mostly smelled of liquor and which made her mouth water. She picked up just her teacup and swallowed all of the tea that was left. "There was this old Bavarian up around Stumptown," she explained to Bianchini, who had all the concern of a friendly drunkard, but would know the common name for the former center of the logging camps. "He used to call me that. He pronounced it different, of course." She said that to Ruby. "But the others took to saying it too, and none of them could say it the same, and turned it to Blue instead." She glanced to Hooper, then faced Bianchini again and gave him a grin. "It means drunk, or so he said."

Bianchini drew his thick brows together while he considered the teacup again, then slowly shook his head. "Sorry, Bl—Batch. That's what I used to hear them call you."

"I know." Batch put the cup down, clanking it on the saucer, but at least quietly this time. "It's not so terrible, and it wasn't wrong, was it?" She looked around the table, to Ruby and the impatient stranger, and then to Hooper. "The tea was good. Thank you."

She nearly sighed in relief when some warmth returned to Hooper's eyes. "Glad to please you, Miss Batch."

Next to Batch, Bianchini gave a start. Batch let her lips turn up in a smile Hooper would see, before looking away.

"Are we playing?" Ruby asked the table at large, drawing most of the attention away from Batch.

Carillo really should marry her. Batch almost said it aloud.

Instead, she stood up, hoping she didn't blush deeper when Hooper half-stood to acknowledge her leaving, and then Bianchini, tipsy and confused, did the same. Batch patted his shoulder, and thought she must be very red from the way Hooper grinned. She nodded to everyone trying to get on with their game.

"I suppose I should leave you to it." She wasn't playing, after all, and someone else would soon want the chair. "Perhaps I'll take a walk before I head home," she added, to just Hooper. "Good night," she told Ruby, and then was unable to be still for any longer, so she left.

The cooler air outside felt wonderful on her warm face, but she had too much fire in her and too many thoughts whirling through her mind for her to stay in one place. She looked in at the jail out of habit, but Tinney and Carillo waved her off, and she was, for the first time in a long while, content to go.

Back out under the night sky, she walked slower, glancing up to the drifting clouds before stopping to roll a cigarette. The strike of a match behind her didn't startle her as it should have, although she did turn to watch Hooper come closer, awed to see her there. Hooper held the flame out for Batch to light her cigarette, and, once that was done, Batch started to walk again, a slow, meandering sort of walk that didn't suit the restlessness Hooper kept sparking in her.

"You don't even like a smoke," she remarked, voice raw but also only for Hooper to hear. "Why do you have those and the papers and everything else?"

Hooper did not quite keep pace with her, staying about two steps behind. "People expect you to do certain things. If you don't want to stand out, you do them." When Batch turned to look pointedly over Hooper's men's getup, Hooper nodded in understanding but didn't laugh. "If you don't want them to notice you even more, or for any other reason," she corrected herself. "It's easier that way."

Batch nodded, then turned back around. "The drink too?" she prompted quietly. "I thought it was the cards, but it isn't, is it?"

"I don't hate a whiskey," Hooper admitted, "but liquor doesn't really affect me. The smoke inside buildings is more of a bother, really." Batch glanced back again in time to see Hooper scratching her nose.

"I can stop." Batch hadn't taken more than one puff of the thing anyway. "I don't actually... It gives me something to do, something to hold. I should just roll them and leave them for Tinney instead of wasting money."

"If you like." Hooper was smiling. Somehow, Batch knew she was. "You might find something else to do someday. With your hands, I mean."

She likely meant something practical, and not what Batch remembered when she thought of Hooper and her hands. Not that Batch could've done any of that in public.

She swallowed. "Do people often drink tea at poker tables where you're from? Or call an overgrown tomboy Miss like it's nothing?" Batch didn't turn. "Or not be called Miss at all if they don't want?"

Hooper touched the back of Batch's arm. "I don't want you to get the impression that it's easy, where I'm from. We have people from all over—welcome people from all over, and are welcomed, and... and that creates some problems, trying to make everyone understand each other and work together. But for the most part...." Batch realized Hooper had stopped and turned to find her gesturing and scowling as she searched for the right words. When Hooper raised her head, for a moment, her eyes seemed to glow with the light from a nearby window. "It's difficult, you see, for everyone there to not know everyone else's business, but we try to make it clear what is private and what might require help from others..." Once again, Batch compared the sound that came out of Hooper to a growl, one more frustrated than furious. "I'm not great with explaining but... lots of those in our town come from places where you get a choice in what people call you, and in who you lov—spend time with. And if other people don't like that..."

"They aren't welcome anymore?" Batch guessed, hoping she seemed calm when she was anything but. She wouldn't call Hooper a liar to her face but that simply could not be true.

Hooper took a step to bring herself closer. Her eyes were narrowed, as if she suspected Batch didn't believe her, but all she said was, "If we were there now, I'd ask to take your arm, and if you allowed it, no one would remark on it, except to wish us a good evening."

A shiver went through Batch. She didn't know if it was fear. She didn't think so, but she couldn't have explained it otherwise. If they had both been in skirts, almost no one would have questioned them being arm in arm. Hooper in pants, as Hooper said she always would be, changed that. Yet it remained possible, according to Hooper, if only in her mysterious hometown.

Batch did not put her arm out. She started to walk again, and when Hooper followed, still a step behind, she slowed until they were nearly side by side. Her stomach flipped and fluttered. If this was fear, it wasn't only fear. She dropped the cigarette and crushed without pausing.

"Does the sky look like this where you come from?" She shouldn't ask about a place she'd never see. She shouldn't believe silly tales, either.

"Oh, bigger, somehow," Hooper answered, and Batch believed her. "There's more of it, except for mountains, but you can go up into the hills and be so close to all those stars you'll find yourself trying to touch 'em."

She let Batch turn onto a side street without comment, and did not venture any closer even when they were alone in a darkened, empty alley or stumbling up the stairs to Batch's room at last. Batch whispered something, a warning, that the hour wasn't late enough for her landlady to be asleep, though she was likely well on her way to being fully soused. Then they were inside, in the dark, and she was against the door with Hooper's hands at her waist beneath her coat and Hooper kissing the side of her neck.

"Batch." Hooper said it like it was torn from her, but Batch was too busy gasping to remark on it. She had her hands under Hooper's coat as well, drawing her in until their bodies were flush and the feel of Hooper's breasts against hers made her writhe a little. It should not have felt as good as it did; Batch very nearly resented it. Hooper held her by her hips without stopping her kisses, dragging her teeth underneath Batch's ear and shuddering when Batch grabbed a handful of her hair to hold her there and knocked Hooper's hat to the floor.

Hooper inhaled deeply, and used her teeth again, to tease, or so Batch thought, until Hooper turned her face to pull in another long breath against Batch's throat. She flattened her hands, urging Batch to be still although she must have felt how Batch's heart was racing. "Please," she whispered finally, as though Batch hadn't reached for her too, as though they were breathing heavy in the dark and wanting each other.

But maybe that wasn't what she meant. Batch kept still though it made her tremble, and waited until Hooper's breathing had calmed some before she spoke, and that was just to say, "I need to get the lamp."

"I'll do it." Hooper didn't move right away despite the offer, kissing Batch's neck again in a few places before groaning and stepping back. She found the lamp without tripping once in the dark, and lit it, her gaze on Batch against the door even before the orange light had spread to the corners of the room.

"Thank you again for the tea." It squeaked out of Batch, made her cough.

Hooper smiled, bright as daybreak. "My pleasure, miss." She came forward, then paused to reach into her coat. "I've got something else for you too."

When she was a step away, she held out her hand, revealing a small wooden hair comb, the kind used to decorate hair more than to help hold it in place. It was dark wood, not polished, with curving lines carved into the top.

Batch stared at it, then looked up. Again, Hooper had her speechless and overwarm. "For me?" she finally asked, when she thought she could.

"Of course." Hooper picked it up to let Batch look at it better. The carved lines were in the shape of a flower, perhaps a rose; Batch would have to look in the morning light. "I made it for you."

That was startling. "You did? When? Not from atop a moving stage."

She got a shrug. "I don't sleep as much as some." Hooper held up the comb. "Do you like it?"

Batch nodded and took it, half-expecting to break it from gripping it too hard. But she slipped it into her hair above her ear and turned her head to let Hooper see the rose nestled there. "Does it look all right? Not silly?"

"Silly?" Hooper echoed before pressing Batch to the door and sighing into her neck. "Batch." She sounded weak. "No, you don't look silly. You look... you look like my..." She pulled in a breath. "You're so lovely I can hardly stand it. That's all. May I kiss you?"

She hadn't asked the last time. Batch didn't know what to feel about the difference. "Of course," she returned at last, and slipped back against the door, eyes closed, wet between her legs and confused about it when she was given one, then several, soft kisses on the mouth. It was only confusing because she didn't feel any need to rush through them despite what the rest of her body said. She put her hands on Hooper's shoulders and one slid down, as if on its own, to cup Hooper's breast over her shirt but beneath her vest.

Batch's thighs were shaking, but she could have stayed where and how she was for much longer. Strange, but she didn't mind. Not until Hooper murmured, "Lovely," and kept kissing her, gentle and slow, as though she didn't feel what Batch did, and Batch, afire, sighed back, "Olivia," in slightly vexed complaint.

She knew she was wrong from how Hooper responded to the name, but forgot her complaints and her impatience, forgot everything but Hooper for some time after that.

She had to keep her hand over her mouth to muffle her cries; Hooper certainly wasn't encouraging her to keep quiet. Batch's use of her name had stirred something in Hooper that Batch had only glimpsed the last time. Hooper had lifted Batch to the bed with no struggle, and removed Batch's clothes with remarkable speed and only one popped button.

Batch was allowed a few moments to touch Hooper in return, slipping a hand down between them until Hooper had growled into her neck and tightened her thighs and urged her on, but for all that, it was Batch under her mouth that drew her special, pleased voice from her again. Or Batch twisting to allow her access to her corset laces. Or leaning over Batch to watch her face while Batch clenched around her fingers and turned her head to try to moan into the pillow.

"How?" Batch panted to her at last, blinking up at Hooper's shining face. "How are you so strong?"

Hooper's eyes went wide. Then she slid her gaze to the side. "Does it bother you?"

Batch looked her over, then grabbed Hooper at her sides and flipped her over like they were two boys wrestling in the dirt. Batch had done her share of wrestling, and fighting dirty, for that matter. She still hadn't expected Hooper to fall so easily. But she stared down at her while catching her breath, and Hooper stared back, nearly glassy-eyed. They were practically against the wall, Batch's knee slipping off the side of the bed. But she didn't move, and Hooper didn't seem capable of it.

Hooper had landed with her hands on either side of her head. Batch leaned down to capture them, although she didn't put much force in it. Hooper just blinked a few times, then slowly tipped her head up. It put her throat on display. Batch decided distractedly that Hooper's throat wasn't nearly as kissed as Batch's was, and that she could remedy that.

So she did.

It didn't make her growl, but it was sweet and warming to suck kisses along Hooper's neck and to hear the sounds Hooper made. It made Batch hot again, after a while, made her damp in good places and perhaps Hooper too.

"I thought you liked the idea of me done up in skirts and petticoats," Batch commented, rolling her hips in way that didn't ease a damn thing but was still agreeable. "Didn't think you'd like this."

"Hmm?" Hooper blinked again. "What? You can do this in skirts. What?" she asked again, looking slightly more aware. "However you please. All of it. You. That. As if you couldn't take me in petticoats." She inhaled, only to exhale longingly. "Oh, you like that, too. Your scent is...."

Batch paused. "Scent?"

Hooper's gaze sharpened. It was Batch's only warning.

Hooper had Batch on her back in the center of the bed again in moments, as if Batch had never pinned her. She crawled down Batch's body to lick her thigh, then sat up to regard Batch heavily. "Scent," she said, voice thick. "Taste. The sound of your heart. My—" she swallowed "my girl, if you will, Batch. My girl, for now."

Batch closed her eyes. "Hooper, you...." She wanted to stay quiet, but no amount of trying could keep her mouth shut now. "You tell stories and I don't believe them, but I wish they were true." Hooper's girl, even only between them, was a thing to make her breath come faster. "I follow anyone who's nice to me. I dream and I dream, with or without whiskey. I'm still Blue, you know. I've gone through a sleeping man's clothes to look for money for drink. And tea!" She looked at Hooper again but couldn't meet her gaze. "Ruby had to show me how to pour it like those ladies do. What are you even doing here? You're something amazing. You don't belong here, in our mess, in this room."

"Do you?"

Batch licked her lips. "It's what I know."

Hooper carelessly brushed her hair out of her face. "I only knew where I grew up. I have some memories of traveling when I was a child. But there, mostly, is what I knew. To leave it was more than a little terrifying, but I wanted to see things. And I had to."

"In order to find your wife?" Batch licked her lips again, had to fight not to sound breathless or to look at Hooper and frown, and imagine her arm in arm with a nice girl, a creature in petticoats who would take her, and kiss her neck, and whisper her name to bring her in close.

"Yeah." Hooper drew Batch's gaze up with a gentle touch to her cheek. Her thumb brushed Batch's lips before she looked Batch in the eye. "Well, to find what felt right, in the manner of my father's side of the family. Which is a twisting path sometimes, and can take sacrifice." Hooper briefly touched the scarring on top of her ear. "It took me in a lot of directions, but I wasn't really impatient until I started to work regularly around the valley. Didn't know why at first." She crooked a smile. "People told me about you. About Batch. I suppose because of how you dress and how I dress. And I was curious, though I wasn't driven yet. But I came here because they said if you weren't up in the camps, you were down here, and I don't like the camps."

"There's something sad about them," Batch agreed quietly. "All those trees being felled at once. All the deaths from working carelessly and too fast."

Hooper nodded. "So I came here. And you—well, Carillo and all the townspeople and farmers who didn't want to do whatever Brannan said—were in a hell of a situation. Which still wasn't my business.

Humans—people often get into messes, and my family, neither side, has benefitted much from getting involved. Usually the opposite."

"But Carillo is Carillo, and you wanted to help," Batch guessed.

With a huff, Hooper went on. "I thought about it, and went to go talk to him, but he wasn't at the jail. In case of trouble, he had you standing guard. Just you, and Tinney helping do the rounds through the streets. But it was you I met. I came up, and you half-pulled your gun, fast. Even barely able to stand, you were fast, and you kept your attention on me even though I could see it taxed you. I knew who you were from the way you dressed, who you had to be. So I said, 'Didn't meant to scare you, Batch. I came to help.' And you said, snarled really, 'When I can't take it, I'll let you know.' Then Tinney came up to calm you down and explain the situation, which I was now a part of." Hooper returned her hand to Batch's cheek. "Because it felt right."

Batch's breath caught in her throat, an embarrassing, strangled sound.

Hooper glanced away. "The rest of it, from my mother's side of the family, well, that took a bit longer. Eulalia and Ruby got you cleaned up, because they thought it would help you feel better, which I think it did, for a while. But you still weren't well, and by then, Carillo didn't want either of them anywhere remotely dangerous. So it was me and Tinney who took turns staying with you, getting you water, wiping your brow to keep you cool." Hooper rubbed her nose, looked back, then away again. "I'm not like my mother, not as good at those matters. You smelled of sickness and sweat, only a little of the soap they used for your bath. But you also finally smelled like you."

"I smell?" It slipped out, a fool question. But then, Batch was a fool who couldn't stop staring at Hooper. Batch had probably rivaled a skunk then. She had a better question. "You helped care for me?"

Hooper shrugged and scratched her nose this time, then finally met Batch's eyes. "For a while, before Carillo needed me elsewhere and Tinney took over watching you. But he promised me he'd protect you with his life." Hooper furrowed her brow. "I'd take him back home too, if I thought he would go. He's good, for a hu—he's good people."

Batch should know when to shut up by now. "Too?"

Hooper twisted her lips into a grimace, then squared her shoulders and took a deep breath. "To be as brave as you, I suppose I must," she said first, making no sense. "If you would allow it, Miss Batch, I would like to court you. Despite this," she gestured between them, both of them naked as could be and eager for more, "my intentions are the purest kind."

Batch stared, and stared, and opened her mouth. Not even a squeak followed. She closed her mouth, then tried again. "Intentions?" she asked faintly

"I don't expect you to have any funny feelings," Hooper assured her, though Batch hadn't mentioned that. "I don't mind waiting, or doing my best to make you feel them."

How strange for the butterflies in Batch's stomach to decide to fly. Hooper was speaking hogwash, her usual fanciful nonsense. Not even Tinney's fairy poem had said anything as bold. Some of the other poems, but not that one.

"I probably should've waited to invite myself to your bed," Hooper admitted, while Batch lay there, dazed and dreaming, "but I spent months keeping my distance and trying to give you time to feel better and maybe.... Well, I spent months, even though I took more work that brought me this way, and you were never around when I was in town. Tinney finally tugged me down by my collar to tell me that I needed to work on my patience, because whatever I thought I was being, it was not that."

Batch decided not to think about Tinney now. She put her hand over Hooper's mouth. "Hooper, I'm no good. I can't even—"

Hooper's breath was warm. Batch forgot what she'd been saying. Hooper tugged Batch's hand away, though she continued to hold it. "I like you, Batch. Never mind the other feelings for now. I like you. Just know that, or work on knowing it, if you can."

There were things others might have done, or said, to that. Blue would have talked for hours, slurring her words, trying to find what would make it better. But Blue would have been arguing to stay, not listening to someone else do the same.

Hooper sighed, perhaps regretful. "When I finally saw you again, you were cleaned up and sitting peacefully with your eyes closed, and I caught your scent from across the room and I... lost my head. Maybe I don't know you all the way yet, but I know a lot, and, well, I like you, Batch."

"Batch is another joke," Batch blurted, then froze. The consequences of even this admission might be too much, she was painfully aware of that. The words came out anyway. "From when I was just a kid. Maybe... maybe too young to be alone." Tinney would have said so, and Tinney knew nearly everything. "A girl dressed like a boy with no manners or... refinements." Another Ruby word. Batch frowned for it. Batch, who could barely read. "'Just like a young bachelor,' they said. It was meant to be a joke. But it was easier, too, to just be Batch, rather than...."

"You don't have to tell me."

Hooper kissed Batch's hand. She was ridiculous. A made-up character from a poem or a dime novel. A hero.

The thought stuck. Batch deepened her frown, then shook her head. "I think I do. For me... for... I'm not really Batch either anymore, am I? Not Blue, not Batch. I'm not sure who I am now."

"I can wait." Hooper leaned down, just a little, as if needing Batch to know she meant it. "Or be here, with you, if you'd rather, while you figure it out. I'll still have to work, but I can visit more and—"

Batch pulled her down and kissed her, square on the mouth, quick where Hooper would have been soft and sweet. But when she released her, Hooper was slow to sit back up and reopen her eyes.

"Primrose," Batch said, watching intently for signs of laughter or mockery. She cleared her throat. "Primrose," she said again, flushed to her toes. "My ma gave me that name. Now that is funny, in the real sense of the word. Me, with a name like that. Primrose Elton, following her father through prospector camps, and then logging camps, and then on her own. Anyone would laugh."

"Primrose." Hooper touched Batch's cheek, her nose, the bow in her upper lip. Her eyes were fierce. Her eyes were bright. Her eyes were beautiful. "Are you going to throw me out now?"

Stunned, Batch shook her head. "Never crossed my mind. Do... do you want me to call you Olivia all the time? Not just when we're like this?"

"Hmm," she could feel Hooper shiver, "call me what you please. But I do like the sound, I admit. And you? What should I call you?"

"I don't know." People would react to hear Batch called by her given name, the same way or worse that they would react to hearing her addressed as Miss Batch. "As you have been, for now." Batch slid her hands up and down Hooper's sides, raising goosebumps. "Except..." She liked how Hooper reacted when she called her Olivia and wanted to know the feeling for herself. "Except maybe, when we're alone, you could use my name?"

Hooper was so clever, and so pretty when something made her happy. "Primrose," she said, tender and soft. "Are you going to refuse my suit?" She traced Batch's lower lip now, brushed her chin, her cheekbone, beneath her ear. "You're well within your rights. I didn't do it as I should have. Although I suspect most don't."

Batch didn't like to see Hooper so uncertain. Hooper shouldn't know shame the way Batch did. She'd done nothing wrong. "I've no complaints about you, Olivia Hooper, even with your tall tales. But I don't believe I'm right, even if your funny feeling tells you so."

"Ah." Hooper seemed relieved. All at once, her manner was easy again, pleased. "That's fine. I get to try to convince you, you see."

"You do?" Batch did not know how to take that, but Hooper's hands were back on her, petting over her shoulders, so she looked up but didn't argue.

Hooper nodded. "That's our way, where I come from. And I do not tell tall tales. I have never lied to you. Not about anything like that. Although, I admit there are things I will need to confess before we go much further." She exhaled roughly. "Hopefully, they won't scare you away."

"I'll also have things to tell you." Batch didn't scowl, there was no point in it, but her stories were not pretty.

Hooper petted Batch's stomach, soothing flutters she could not possibly have known where there unless she had them too. "I heard all about you before I ever met you, and I know better than to believe everything I hear. I also know even if every store were true, it doesn't change anything for me. But I will listen to whatever you decide to tell me. I'm not as good a listener as Tin, but I'm learning."

"You're too good," Batch sighed at her. "You're like him."

"I am not good," Hooper countered. "I've acted selfishly, really. You make me feel all kinds of greedy, possessive things. My mother's side of the family is often like that." She seemed offended when Batch raised her eyebrows doubtfully. "I was grateful they were there to give you aid, but I wanted to stand guard over you so Ruby and Eulalia couldn't touch you." Hooper briefly hung her head. "It was a childish wish, but I had it. I could hear my mother scolding me... Olivia Hooper, you're better than that! You are more than your wild nature! Then I finally got to talk to you again and I nearly drove you off by inviting myself to see your room." She shook her head. "I'll make more mistakes."

Batch hardly had the right to hold anyone else's mistakes against them, if she even noticed them. "Your biggest one is right here. I'm still not—Batch is still not a wife. Your town of kind oddities can't change that."

"Kind oddities." Hooper snorted, amused, before leaning down against until they were almost nose to nose. "I will bring you gifts, and I will walk with you, and I will kiss you plenty. And when you are convinced, I will carry you off like they say fairies used to do, and I will build you a house below the hills that will not be fancy, but I will at least manage a bigger bed."

At the mention of fairies, Batch nearly asked if Hooper had been reading the same poems as Tinney, but the rest of Hooper's speech stopped her. "Hogwash," she said at last, but faintly.

"Or, if you don't want that, we can get a place in town. A house or a few rooms. If you don't like my town, we could go elsewhere." Hooper regarded her seriously. "As long as I get to visit my family."

The lump in Batch's throat was tears. She gulped air and swallowed but they wouldn't stay down. She covered her mouth with one hand.

Hooper sat up, alarmed. "I made you cry?"

Batch shook her head, although she was crying, water spilling from her eyes without her permission. Batch was crazy, and she was tough, and she drank and got in fights, but she did not cry. Yet of course, here she was, sobbing behind her hand while Hooper grew more and more worried.

"You aren't supposed to cry!" she fretted, and this time, it was a laugh which unexpectedly spilled out of Batch.

They stilled, the two of them together, and stared at one another.

"I don't actually know what I'm doing," Hooper admitted, sheepish, calming slightly when Batch shuddered but took her hand from her mouth. "I'm not lying, but I am pretending, a bit. You're my ma—girl—that hasn't changed unless you want it to." She carefully wiped some of the tears from Batch's cheek. "Please don't cry. Tinney will have my hide."

Batch didn't even know what had caused the tears in the first place. "A future," she croaked, and shook her head again, not wanting to explain. She put her hands on Hooper again, stroking her back and marveling at how Hooper managed to stay so soft while living as she did. She pulled as gently as she knew how, which wasn't much, and Hooper came down to lie on top of her, then roll onto her side when Batch grunted.

Hooper put her face to Batch's shoulder, hiding against her neck.

Batch swallowed a few times, throat tight, the pressure in her chest slowly easing. The ceiling was orange in the lamplight, plain. She supposed ordinary people, even proper ladies, did not have paintings on their ceilings, or windows to look up at the sky.

"Sometimes, could we sleep outside, to look up at the moon?" she asked, shivering when Hooper exhaled a half-laugh.

"Someday, I will tell you how charming I find it that you admire the moon, and why." Hooper rubbed the tip of her nose against Batch's skin, then into her hair. "And yes, if you like. Though it might shock Tinney when I end up loving you in the moonlight."

She'd decided to bring Tinney along anyway. Batch briefly wondered what Tinney would have to say about that. Then she wriggled her hand beneath Hooper until her hand was free, and brought it up to stroke the shell of Hooper's ear.

She took a deep, shaky breath.

"Tell me about your town again."

Epilogue

OLIVIA stopped at the base of the steps leading down from the jail, staring at a dark and mostly empty street. She could see the lights from the hotel and imagined its warmth, then shivered as some water somehow got past her hat and coat and trickled down the back of her neck.

At the drag of Tinney's foot on the floor, his slight indrawn breath like he had something to say, she turned around. Tinney stood in the jailhouse doorway, safely under the overhanging roof and therefore protected from the late spring rain.

He was not a large man. Had likely not been when younger, either. Olivia's father would stand taller than him, and the elves Olivia knew were not known for their height. He also did not quite have a scent like most other human men, even the older ones, but the whys of that were really none of Olivia's business.

With the light from inside behind him, his expression was difficult to read, but his tone wasn't.

"It's raining, if you hadn't noticed."

Olivia grunted, which Tinney couldn't hear over the sound downpour anyway.

He was standing near where Batch had stood just over a year ago when Olivia had met her. Finally met her. The Batch of so many stories and jokes—although, joshing or not, most people had warned Olivia not to make the jokes where Batch could hear, not unless Olivia wanted cracked ribs or a busted nose.

Batch was ferocious when riled, something that embarrassed her, but which a part of Olivia, the part that had howled upon meeting Batch, recognized and admired.

That night, it hadn't been raining.

Olivia blinked, then tossed her head to shake off the memory of Batch rising from a chair outside the door, one hand tight on the post supporting the roof so she could stay on her feet.

A human probably wouldn't have noticed her there, nowhere near a window, half-hidden on the shadowed porch at night. It had probably been Batch's plan to surprise anyone trying to sneak inside the small building to lie in wait for Carillo or to take the rifles stored inside. A good plan for someone who'd known she wasn't in a good way and wouldn't do well in a more direct or prolonged confrontation.

To Olivia's eyes, the Batch of local legend had been an unsteady figure, with her hair messily pinned back and her shirt buttoned wrong. Her hair hadn't shined then like it shined now. But her gaze had still been sharp, at least in that moment.

Olivia looked at Tinney as though her heart wasn't pounding. She remembered she was supposed to speak. "I know it's raining!" she shouted back. "Maybe I like it! Maybe it saves me the money for a bath!"

She shouted to be heard by human ears, but the rain had emptied the street. Or, she should say, the mud had. In the winter, the dirt roads were nearly impassable for the stages. Thankfully, this rain hadn't gone on long enough and the stage had come into town just fine.

"Wasting time!" Tinney charged back. He should return to sitting by the pot-bellied stove to keep his bones from aching in this weather, not needling Olivia over her choices. He never spoke like this to Batch. "I thought you had someplace you'd rather be," he added, too pointedly, too knowing.

Of course, after the last half hour in his presence, Olivia suspected Tinney knew everything on her mind. She didn't know what Batch would feel about that, but there was no helping it. Tinney was kind, in his way, and wise. Not inclined to lie as most humans seemed to do as naturally as breathing. Nothing against lying. It was useful, at times, but Olivia thought humans could stand to do less of it. They denied a lot of things that there was simply no use in denying.

But not Old Tin, as Batch sometimes called him.

Olivia finally gave him a nod and hoped she didn't look too anxious as she made herself turn and start walking. Her hat kept her face somewhat dry, and her long coat was doing its job, but she had been in the rain for most of the day, and her time in the jail with Tinney by the stove hadn't dried the rest of her much. Olivia could take a lot of discomfort, more than most, but her toes were freezing inside her boots.

Strange that Batch in her younger years would have chosen someone like Tinney for a friend since he could be unflinching. But then again, Batch was always braver than she thought she was. Her mate seemed to think bravery only involved fights or bloodshed or things of that ilk. It was confusing, but somehow charming, like so many things about Batch.

Because of Tinney more than the rain, Olivia did not slow her pace, although she truly didn't know what awaited her in the hotel. Tin had made it clear, in his way, that there was a situation, and it was not only in Olivia's mind, and that she needed to resolve it. He had not clarified the nature of the situation, however. Olivia had met one seer in her travels, hiding from the world in the graveyards outside Los Cerros, but she suspected that seer and Tin would get along just fine.

Lots of warnings and hints, no useful information. Really, all Tinney had done was tell Olivia to go see Batch, which was meaningless since Olivia always wanted to see Batch. That was why she'd traded jobs with a friend and hurried back here earlier than she was expected to, and gone first to Batch's room and then the jail to look for her. If Batch wasn't in either of those places, then it was very likely she was somewhere around the St. Cristopher, talking to Ruby or Eulalia or taking on more of the odd jobs she'd been doing for them. In exchange for meals, she claimed, with her heart skipping and her cheeks going dark.

That didn't mean anything. It was a lie, sure, but Batch did that when embarrassed, and one of the few things that ever truly embarrassed her was the list in her head of stuff she thought a lady should know.

Olivia imagined it that way, lady, not woman or girl. That was how she figured Batch viewed it. A lady, or, at least, a different version of woman, was what Batch had secretly longed to be despite her rough edges, and she worried over things that had been denied her through no fault of her own. Olivia couldn't begrudge her that, even though she hadn't been denied them, she just wanted nothing to do with them.

Well, she wanted nothing to do with them for herself. Olivia put a hand to her warming face as she thought back to her talk with Tinney in the jail, and the sewing basket on the desk that quite obviously didn't belong to Tin. She didn't mind if Batch wanted to explore all of that. She more than didn't mind.

It was a far cry from Olivia's first sight of her, or even from the shock a few days later of realizing what Batch was to her. Or even Batch when Olivia had finally seen her sober and at peace. But each change made Batch blush and cast furtive looks Olivia's way, uncertain, and showering her in compliments was no hardship. Pleasing, really. Olivia liked to give Batch things. It was one of the earliest realizations she'd had about their courtship and her prickly mate. Nobody had ever given Batch anything soft or beautiful.

From what Tinney had said, and Carillo had implied with frowning silence, nobody had given Batch anything but grief for most of her life, forgetting her and denying her care, or making her a joke and turning her into the sort of person to swing at the slightest provocation.

She could still swing, Olivia suspected, but was less inclined to now. Olivia had taken it as a sign that Batch was feeling happy and that Olivia had been doing well in her courting.

Her steps slowed, not only because of the mud. The fight—no, it hadn't been a fight, but something had upset Batch when Olivia had last been in town. Batch had regarded her without speaking, vanished when Olivia had hoped to dine with her, turned up again to kiss her hungrily, and then insisted Olivia must have someplace else to be and all but tossed her out the door.

It was the kind of thing to leave younger wolves baying at the moon in bewildered despair. Olivia hadn't done that, but it had been a close thing. She'd been hurt, and then worried, and then so anxious she hadn't been able to wait for her scheduled route that would bring her back to this area.

They'd told her. Everyone on her mother's side of the family had told her that mates were never guaranteed, even if you found them. Humans in particular were fragile, and when they weren't falling ill, they were making rash choices or living with doubts that no one like Olivia could ever fully understand.

Despite her hesitation, she reached the hotel, and walked up the steps to the porch before pausing again. The main room was bustling, although not especially rowdy. Olivia was escorting a rather sedate group up to the geysers, although they all still liked to stop off for one last night of good food and drink before their health treatments.

That's what Olivia had been doing in town last time as well, escorting more of them up there. Batch worried about the danger, but with everything in the area resolving itself into farmland and even the logging crews packing up and leaving, there weren't huge amounts of money to be found on most of the stages. Didn't mean people wouldn't try, but it was steady work, anyway, and it kept Olivia around while she waited and courted and waited some more.

No one in her mother's family had mentioned how long waiting could take. Olivia had been under the impression human courtships did not take months like this. Perhaps she'd been mistaken.

With a sigh, she went to the entrance and stepped inside. Even with experience in actual cities, it took her a moment to calm her senses down in a room full of humans to focus only on what she needed to.

In other towns, she slept near the stage more often than not. It saved money, it was quieter, and she didn't mind sleeping on the ground and coming in to eat and clean up, or, back before finding Batch, maybe charming a girl to pass the time. But since finding her mate and being given the privilege of knowing Batch intimately, Olivia slept there, with her, instead of anywhere else.

Now she wondered if she should have asked Eulalia or John for a room here for the night, or just plan on heading out to the stage instead of presuming she was welcome elsewhere.

Tinney had marched her toward this, she reminded herself. Tinney wasn't cruel. He had watched Olivia poke around the front room of the jail and do her best to not stare at the fabric spilling out of that sewing basket, before he'd finally asked why the hell Olivia was wasting time with him instead of seeking out her Primrose.

It gave her a jolt even to remember it. She wasn't sure what was more shocking, Tinney telling her that he knew exactly how Olivia regarded

Batch and implying some kind of approval, or Tinney using the name Primrose.

Batch must have told him.

That was good, surely. But... Olivia had felt blessed, for a while, to be the only one who knew.

But that was out now, along with the parts of Olivia's desires that these sorts of humans usually frowned upon. At least, that much was out and known to Tinney.

Quite probably to Ruby as well. Olivia strangely felt no fear at the prospect. Ruby, like the card player she was, did not reveal much if she didn't want to. But she saw a lot, and she noticed things, and Batch was often caught staring when Olivia was around.

"Got good news, Hooper?" Bill called out from behind the bar, and Olivia realized she was smiling to herself like a lovestruck fool.

"No, but I'm hoping for a good night!" she called back as playfully as she could manage. For all that, she didn't stop, not at the bar, not over at the table where Ruby would end up as soon as any sort of card game started. Although there was no sign of her at present, or Batch for that matter.

Olivia offered a friendly, if distracted, greeting to John, and then headed toward the bath room. Batch would spend all her pay on hot water if she could, and if she wasn't set to refuse Olivia outright, Olivia was going to find the biggest tub she could for their future home. She might even look into how the hotels in the city managed their heated water so Batch could have baths without much fuss. Batch might want to marry her for that alone, but Olivia had a cousin who made oils and soaps to sell, and Olivia could offer her those too.

The bath room was unoccupied. Olivia briefly contemplated a bath. Trading jobs to get back here faster hadn't given her much time to rest or get clean. Even a warm water bath would take the chill from her toes, and she'd like to look presentable when she did finally find Batch. But she wanted to see Batch more, so she continued on.

Perhaps if she just saw her, it would let her breathe a little at last and stop thinking the worst.

It might have been the mud on her boots or the water in her lashes that made the group of ladies at a table in the corner stare at her when she reemerged into the main room. Olivia tipped her hat at them politely, only to remember she had her hat on and hurriedly remove it, leaving it, and then her soaked coat, with Bill rather than on the stand by the door.

Batch had her flustered but good.

It would have been nice to see Ruby, who would have smiled her secret smiles but given Olivia an idea as to Batch's mood. Last time, Olivia didn't know what she'd done wrong, if anything, and hadn't had a chance to hint around to Ruby about it.

Maybe her revelations to Batch had finally sunk in. That was what had haunted Olivia for the past three nights when she couldn't sleep.

After all, it had taken Olivia sitting in front of Batch on four furry legs, and then trying to demonstrate how quickly she healed, to even make Batch believe her when Olivia had told her the truth of her parentage and her families. It shouldn't have been that much of a surprise, she'd thought, after weeks of telling Batch how her hometown worked and what they believed in. But Batch had looked faint, and asked only one or two questions, and after that had mostly avoided the subject.

But she hadn't run away screaming, and she hadn't refused Olivia her company in bed or out of it, so Olivia had taken hope. So much that she had mentioned more of the rest of it. The most important part of it all. The crucial bit.

My mate, whispered into Batch's skin, and placed with kisses along her thighs, and murmured against her ears over and over until Olivia thought Batch understood.

Perhaps she didn't, and she thought Olivia was talking nonsense.

Perhaps she did, and didn't want it.

Of course, at that point in her fretting, Olivia usually remembered that she was thinking about Batch. Batch. The bravest creature to walk in this town. Whether or not Batch understood or wanted it wouldn't matter if Batch didn't think such a thing was meant for someone like her.

"Mate?" Batch had said once, sitting across from Olivia with her mending in her lap while Olivia had cleaned her work gun.

Olivia had thought there was a question in it, so she'd raised her head. But Batch had been frowning down at her sewing by then, and hadn't mentioned anything else.

So, Batch had also been fretting. Tin would have an opinion on that. So would Ruby.

Olivia stopped by the bar, wishing she could drown her sorrows as humans could, then recalling that drinking to avoid a problem never actually seemed to work, despite what humans insisted.

"Ruby around?" she asked Bill when he had a moment. He watched Batch sometimes, but in a wistful way, not covetous. Olivia couldn't mind that when she knew she did it too.

"Upstairs," he filled her in, but with a nod toward the stairs, as if it was all right for Olivia to go and look for herself.

She had no idea what room was Ruby's, although Bill didn't know that. But Olivia could probably sniff it out if she couldn't hear it, so she thanked him and went up.

The trouble hadn't eased her mind any. There were traces of Batch's scent downstairs, but that meant nothing with Batch working here sometimes, or coming in to grab something to eat. Someone pure wolf, or old wolf, might have been able to track Batch from that. But Olivia wasn't from that kind of stock and preferred to use her ears, anyway.

The second floor had more movement, muffled voices, soft footsteps. Olivia came to the landing and around the corner, then froze to see

Carillo holding a large, overloaded tray with both hands and heading her way.

When he saw her, he stopped.

"Hoop." He inclined his head without tipping the tray. "You're back early." He regarded Olivia for another moment, using silence as he liked to, before explaining, "Ruby doesn't feel well, so I brought her some food. Someone from the stage also didn't want to come down for dinner. I said I'd also bring theirs up. I do, sometimes."

Which Olivia had known, but she had thought it more like a favor to John and Eulalia and the staff. Now, she wasn't sure. Carillo had a towel over one arm and no obvious weapons on him—although Olivia wouldn't swear that he was unarmed. He also had his chin up and was watching her carefully.

She frowned in distracted confusion. "Aren't they going to set up a town charter or something? Tinney was ranting about something like that a while back. I thought you'd wind up working for the town. Properly, I mean." Although, now that she thought it over, Batch had been making exasperated noises about the future of the town and its more prominent citizens for a while now.

Carillo didn't shrug, or even blink. He wouldn't blink if a stampede of wild horses came barreling toward him. "They have to name the place first. Too many people fighting over putting their surname on it for anything else to get done."

Granted, Olivia stayed out of politicking in the human world, but from what she understood, Carillo was from the equivalent of the old wolf families around here, and something of a hero to boot. "You're not involved in that?"

Carillo looked like he wanted to scratch the back of his neck. "Ruby says if I want to, then I should act now." He finally blinked. "I don't want to."

Olivia smiled despite her anxiety. "Don't think I blame you," she told him. "But... this?" Carillo was not someone to take orders unless they were sensible and from someone he respected.

He moved his shoulders in a careful shrug. "It fills time and it's honest work. I might not have thought so when I was young, but I thought a lot of foolish things then." He frowned and let her see him do it. "There will be people who will enjoy seeing me do this too much."

Bullies existed everywhere. Even Olivia had grown up knowing some.

Maybe she ought to tell Batch that, help her get over her idea that Olivia's hometown was too good for her, or whatever she fretted about over her mending.

Maybe... maybe Olivia ought to invite some of Batch's family there to join them, in case Batch was somehow worried about that as well. Carillo and Ruby, they were good pack, good people.

Olivia took the tray from Carillo to give his arms a break, and Carillo watched her do it and said nothing.

She cleared her throat. "Ever consider starting out somewhere else?" She did her best to seem offhand and not at all worried over the future and her mate's tender heart. Olivia had no idea what Carillo would think of what she and Batch did together in Batch's little room, much less the rest of it, wolves, and people the humans called elves, and magic and the like. But he was good pack, she reminded herself, and he cared for Batch. She cleared her throat again and became convinced that Carillo allowed himself only a few blinks a year. "If she were to leave, she would miss you."

She didn't say who 'she' was, or why Batch might leave, but Carillo used up another blink.

"I would miss her." A strange expression crossed his face, then he shook his head. "But it's not like that, what you're thinking."

"Oh, no, no. I know that." Olivia stuck the tray on a table, nearly displacing a vase. Batch had said a lot in her feverish dreams while sobering up, enough for Olivia to get some idea of how Batch thought of Carillo, but Olivia had a wolf's nose and a lover's interest enough to know that Batch did not harbor romantic feelings for Mariano Carillo anymore. And whatever she'd had before had been hero worship more than anything. Olivia looked over, frowning now at the suspicion that Carillo knew more than he was telling her. "She'll miss you all the same," she went on, slowly.

Carillo gestured behind him, to either his room or Ruby's or perhaps their shared room, by now, if Eulalia allowed that level of open impropriety. "Ruby's got to earn a living."

His concern was over Ruby, not himself? Olivia gave him a quick grin. "Pretty sure she's adaptable. Remade herself a few times, I'll bet."

He didn't respond to that, not out loud. If Olivia took a good sniff, she could probably figure out his answer. Batch would likely read all sorts of meanings in the quiet.

Olivia stood it for a moment, then scratched her nose and gave up. "Have you seen her around? Batch, I mean? She's not at the jail. She working?"

"No." Carillo gave Olivia a puzzled look, his eyebrows drawing together, then smoothing out. "Those paying us decided there was no longer a need for an extra body. It's just me and Tin, for now."

"Oh." Batch had either been chosen because a woman in pants with a gun didn't suit the town's new image or she'd left so Tin could stay on. Olivia was halfway to smiling fondly over that before she realized that this wasn't a new development, and that was why Carillo had frowned. "How long ago was this?"

Carillo exhaled softly. "Officially, a few weeks now. But she knew it was coming. We all did."

And yet Batch hadn't mentioned it to Olivia. Olivia had a feeling that realization was all over her face because Carillo responded nearly like a wolf would, with deliberate and understanding silence.

But he was still human. "I think," he said carefully, "some things, Batch insists on doing by herself, even when she shouldn't."

Despite the use of human words, it was a fairly pack sentiment. Carillo would fit right in with Olivia's aunts and uncles.

It was a distracted thought.

"So, that's what she's been... the same as you? Odd jobs around the hotel?"

"Not odd jobs but, yes." Carillo gave Olivia another frown, or possibly it was for Batch, and jerked his head toward the end of the hall. He raised his eyebrows, which was more expression than Olivia was used to seeing from him, and then, with a nod, took the tray and continued on downstairs.

It was not quite like being directed onward by Tinney's sharp tongue, but it felt the same.

Olivia truly must've hurt Batch the last time she was here, although how, she still couldn't imagine. It had been going well, if slow, to her mind.

Batch would probably have something to say about that.

It was admittedly hard to judge her sometimes, even when Olivia could smell how much Batch wanted her or hear Batch's heart kick when Batch saw her. Perhaps Olivia should have told her more, the rest of it, and then Batch would finally understand and accept what she was to her.

But if Olivia told her about the consequences of a refusal—which she had not done only because she didn't want to make Batch feel awful for saying no—she suspected Batch would frown at her, and sit with that knowledge for a while, and then wonder why creatures so frightening and big and tough would be nearly killed by something humans dealt with all the time.

"Hearts break over everything," Batch had said once, softly, while Olivia had been dozing and enjoying a rare morning spent together with nowhere to be and nothing to do. "All the time, even if you deny it or try to drown it. I... Sorry. Tinney's been reading his poems again."

She also still dismissed half of Olivia's stories from home as tall tales. Although she listened, barely breathing, wide-eyed, to all of them, and asked to hear a few again.

People should not have broken Batch's heart so much. They wouldn't, in the future, if Olivia had anything to say about it.

Batch was no longer an unofficial deputy and was now doing chores around the hotel. She must have been embarrassed for her to hide it like this. Batch regarded her steady employment as one of the few points of pride in her life.

Squaring her shoulders, Olivia set off down the hall to find her mate and hopefully win her back. But she stuttered to an awkward halt when the door at the end of the hall opened, and a woman came out, already turning to shut the door behind her, one arm full of laundry.

The beat of the heart and the shining brown waves of hair said clearly who it was, and yet Olivia heard herself saying, "Terribly sorry, miss, I must have been steered wrong..." before falling off into stunned silence when Batch spun around to face her.

Olivia had known Batch had ideas, ludicrous notions about what she was allowed to wear and what was too good or graceful or fine for her. She'd known that Batch privately yearned for those things anyway and had vowed to make sure she had them.

Batch had beaten her to it.

She was in a skirt. Skirts, likely, since, from the fall of them, Batch had at least one petticoat on and perhaps a pad at the back. The top skirt was brown plaid, serviceable, maybe even reused or refashioned to fit her. Someone's sturdy old walking skirt that fell around her ankles, revealing delicate black boots with a small heel. She had no gun belt, which was in itself startling, and in its place was an apron. Above that, she wore a cream blouse with slightly puffed shoulders. Batch always pinned her hair up, but generally simply, although she'd said she had a gift for it and had often done the girls' hair in the house where she had briefly worked.

Olivia had thought of those girls asking for Batch's hands on them and felt jealousy, thinking they had done so as a ploy. They may have, but it was clear now that Batch had a way with curls and pins and such. With her hair brushed to softness and pinned up loosely to leave wisps at her nape and at her forehead, she was so beautiful that Olivia worried faintly that Batch would want nothing to do with her now, as so many suitors would come calling.

She swallowed, then met Batch's stare. This was the Batch that might have been, if the world had been kinder. Batch would mutter all kinds of things about her appearance, disparaging comments about freckles from the sun and cheeks stained red, and the little belly she said the whiskey had given her, and how she still needed more meat on her bones after drinking her meals for so long, but Olivia knew that Batch would have no shortage of attention and offers in a growing town like this one. She was too lovely not to.

And Olivia was supposed to convince her to go to a small town in the middle of nowhere, surrounded by creatures Batch wasn't sure about, leaving all her people here unless Olivia could convince them otherwise?

She let out a despairing sigh.

Batch reached up as if to touch her hair. "Do you not like it?" she worried aloud, and bit her lower lip as if Olivia's opinion mattered so very much. She dropped her hands to fuss with her skirt instead, offering a hint of white petticoat and dark stockings.

Olivia whimpered, she was not ashamed to admit it.

Even if she had been, she would have done it again for the way Batch brightened.

"Really?" she asked, shy as a courtly maiden, and gave Olivia a smile that had Olivia stumbling forward without thinking. "I wasn't sure you would come back after the way I was," she added, making Olivia stop short. "It used to drive people off when I acted like that, or annoy them. I didn't even mean to do it, and then I was... I'm sorry. You left, and I thought maybe I'd finally..."

"No." Olivia couldn't let her finish that.

But it didn't reassure Batch like she'd hoped. Batch frowned at the floor and whispered, "Because of that mate notion of yours. You had to come back."

Olivia's lungs were working, but she couldn't manage to form words for several moments, and then just, "I knew I didn't explain it right."

Batch made to cross her arms, then seemed to remember the laundry. She addressed the wall this time, which at least wasn't the floor. "You deserve more than a funny feeling and a girl who can't even control herself." She grimaced. Even that was lovely. "I was set to brawl. Only seeing Ruby's disapproving face stopped me. You must have been so embarrassed."

Olivia genuinely had no idea what Batch was talking about. "I'm sorry. I raced to get back here sooner and maybe I'm a little tired. What? What brawl?"

With a huff, Batch finally looked at her. Her gaze made Olivia want to howl, and she'd always had a rather reedy howl. "That woman. Lady. Girl. Someone. Now that I'm looking for it, I can see... Maybe she didn't know what she was doing. Maybe she did. But she was eyeing you and smiling, and she was pretty and soft-handed, and you were talking to her, and I was a fool who stormed out because if I'd stayed...."

"Oh." Olivia vaguely recalled the daughter of one of the matrons headed up to the resort paying her some close attention. She also recalled barely glimpsing Batch inside the hotel that evening. "That's why you were mad—I mean, upset last time? You were jealous?"

Batch put her chin in the air, and Olivia distantly wondered who had taught her to do that instead of raising her fists for a fight. "No call to look so pleased."

"I'm not." It was a lie, so Olivia went on and tried to make her grin vanish. "Well, it's difficult to explain. You wanting me for yourself is a nice idea, deep down inside. I can admit that. But...You don't need to be, is all. You must know that."

Again, Batch did not seem appeased. "Because of your mate notion."

Olivia's grin disappeared for real. "Please stop calling it that. It's not a notion. It's a certainty. And it's you."

"It's bunk." Batch took a step toward Olivia, and her eyes were big and sad. "It's got to be, because as I am, I wouldn't be a good wife. You might regret it. I can walk away whenever I like. Even if somehow we got wedded in a church, I would leave if I wanted. But you'd be stuck wanting me. I'm trying my best, but I'm still not…" Some of the spirit left her. "I want to be better than this, and yet, I nearly ripped that girl's curls from her head because she was all that I'm not and you smiled at her."

"First of all," Olivia said into the silence afterward, her heart threatening to leap out of her chest, "if you tell me you might leave me, don't expect me to be calm. Second, I don't know how you're thinking of it, but a good wife to me is one who loves me and treats me well, and I hope to be the same to you. I do. And third…" She'd known Batch had gotten into more than her share of fights once upon a time, easily riled, but perhaps also right to be with how some treated her. But Olivia, unfortunately, could only feel pleased. Her mother would be so disappointed. "You were gonna fight for me? Wait. No." She shook her head. "Never mind that for now. I… I came running back here as soon as I could because I thought you were angry with me and I had to know why. And then I find this—" she gestured to Batch's outfit "—which snatched all the clean thoughts right from my head. And then you try to tell me…."

What was Batch trying to tell her? Olivia took a moment to consider the situation, even though she could catch Batch's anxious scent now, thick with roses and the hint of lavender always in her clothes.

"You know I think you're lovely." Olivia's voice was husky, and she made it low, although there was no one else around to hear, or at least, no movement in any of the rooms. "You don't have to change anything for me, or do anything, or…." Her chest went tight, as it had when she had first seen the spill of fabric out of that sewing basket. "I saw your sewing. Your, um, trousseau."

Batch's heart went wild. Her eyes were wide. But she dropped her shoulders and turned her face away. "I never… Esperanza has been working on hers since she first learned to hold a needle, and she was speaking of it, and I thought, I should practice. Have a real skill. And it's not just for weddings and brides!" She turned back to Olivia with a determined, justified air. "It's good to have napkins and handkerchiefs for your home. Or as gifts to give to others. And I could use the practice, truly."

She poked at the laundry, some hotel guest's shirts, then frowned a little, perhaps because Olivia was staring at her with her mouth open. "Tinney helped me order some patterns from the newspaper ads, and he puzzles over the numbers in them with me. He reads to me, sometimes, while I sit with him and sew. It's nice."

"It really is a trousseau?" Olivia couldn't help the question. Tinney hadn't named it so boldly but Olivia had sisters, cousins, friends. She knew why some girls set aside time to make household linens and things, and Tinney had made comments about futures and girls being prepared. But she hadn't expected… "Really?"

Batch returned to scowling at the laundry. "Nothing too fancy," she said at last. "Esperanza gave me some handkerchiefs from hers once she saw what I was about, although she doesn't know why I was thinking of it. Or," Batch's scowl briefly deepened, "I don't think she does. She started to show me the idea behind embroidery, but that's… I'm not the kind of girl to put roses on anything."

She should have roses on everything, Olivia decided, and crept closer while Batch continued to worry aloud. "Ruby is no help. She says she can sew buttons and fix a hem if she must, but that it was never a gift of hers, or even that she likes it." Batch turned to her, eyes sparkling. "Kind of like you. Esperanza and Eulalia say a trousseau is items for your home, for your future. Napkins and tablecloths, apparently. Quilts or lace if you can do that. New clothing." Batch didn't seem to know what to make of Olivia's slow approach or serious expression. Olivia had to fight to be serious or she would coo over Batch sewing roses onto her handkerchiefs or chuckle at the image of her and Tinney pouring over mail-order patterns together. Batch kept talking. "That's trickier, the clothes. Skirts and undergarments. Eulalia told me she'd get me a good length of black or green ribbon so I can at least make my chemises prettier. But then I have to learn to work with that as well."

"I can sew," Olivia volunteered, reluctantly but sincerely. "I don't much like it, but if you needed help, I could at least do the plain bits. If Tinney can do it, I can do it." Olivia's mate needed her, and Olivia was, after all, her father's daughter; elves tended to work quickly and well. "My family is gifted that way, on my father's side." She touched her ear, reminding Batch of her heritage, only to realize her hair had gotten damp despite her hat. But that was a problem for another time.

Batch turned the scowl on her. "It's supposed to be a surprise… I think. Or something like that."

"A surprise?" Olivia echoed, failing to understand until suddenly, she did. A surprise for her. "Oh." All the stars in the sky and the full moon itself were nowhere near as bright as the feeling in her chest. "Oh, you mean to say yes."

Batch stared at her, scowl slowly easing away. Then she swallowed. She was nervous.

Olivia was nervous. Shaking with it. On fire. She inched closer but stopping at the hitch in Batch's breathing.

Olivia briefly closed her eyes and tried to think of anything that might let her be calm. It was important to be calm. Batch was counting on her. If Olivia wasn't calm, she might do something that might shock Batch, like bite Batch's neck for the world to see instead of beneath her skirts for only Olivia to dream about. That thought did not help Olivia any, but knowing that she could talk about it with Batch, with her mate, if she was calm enough, did.

She pulled in a long breath, then opened her eyes. "Linens for our household would be nice, my sweet Miss Primrose, but that's not why I want you—and not that 'mate notion' business again, if you please. Mate... that's just... the feeling telling me to pay attention to this one. To you. The rest was... it wasn't just me courting here. You've been courting me as well."

Batch dared to be surprised. "I have?"

Now, Olivia got to step close. "Oh yes. You shared your secret self with me first. And I am glad to taste your recipes and your attempts to learn new ones, and to see your... well, I saw the spool of scarlet ribbon in your sewing basket. Is that something for me as well, Miss Primrose?"

The way Batch looked when called by her name never failed to make Olivia want to kiss her.

Batch didn't nod or say yes. She said, "Eulalia told me a girl puts things for her wedding night in her trousseau, so if I ever had one, I should have that. Of course, then she looked embarrassed, because it isn't as though my wedding night would be my first time the way it probably was for her."

"Your wedding night?" Oh, Olivia might bite her then, leave marks all over Batch for her whole town to see. Or just keep Batch away for the whole month the way people were supposed to do. The waxing and waning of one whole moon spent in the sweetness of Batch's arms.

She had Batch flustered now. Olivia snuck forward again. Batch didn't stop her or even suggest that she ought to. She just complained, "You're all wet and mud," with a tone already so like an exasperated wife that Olivia could not stand going without touching her any longer.

She spared a moment to listen to make sure and the room Batch had just come from was empty. Batch let herself be walked backward, or maybe it was that she pulled Olivia into the room with her, one hand on her shirt; Olivia didn't care to figure out which.

The door shut behind them. The room had one lamp on, the light low. The laundry fell to the floor. Olivia turned them to get Batch's back to the door and then kissed her without knowing where to put her hands except the side of Batch's face and the hint of her neck bared above her blouse's high collar.

"You're damp," Batch whispered when Olivia had moved on to kiss her beneath her chin and a ticklish spot beneath one ear.

"I rushed to get back here." Olivia's voice went a bit higher than it should have, but Batch had curled a finger into her belt and it felt like they'd been apart for weeks, not days. "Thought you were mad at me." She didn't bite, but she scraped her teeth lightly over soft, rose-and-soap clean skin, exactly how she wished Batch would do to her and how sometimes Batch did.

"Mad at you?" Batch was astonished and breathless. She pulled on Olivia's hair, drawing harsher breathing from her but also making Olivia raise her head. Batch was worrying her lip. "I don't mind you smiling freely at other girls, it's just... that one."

Olivia kissed her to make her quit her fretting. "She made you think I wanted a lady?" she asked softly, touching any inch of Batch's skin she could find. "I do." Batch flinched. Olivia shushed her with another kiss, though only a small one. "I must have. I found you." She stroked Batch's cheek until Batch met her eyes. "I want to bury myself in your scent," she confessed, careful, because she still did not know what Batch thought of her true nature. "But I'm scared of disturbing your pretty hair, or getting my filthy hands on your nice skirt."

"The fabric is dark," Batch told her, serious and quiet, "I don't think it will show."

Olivia pressed her to the door until she could feel unfamiliar stays, perhaps boning, beneath Batch's blouse. For several moments, she had to clench her jaw to keep from making the sounds she wanted to make. "New corset?" she inquired weakly.

"I'm wearing stockings too," Batch answered, a breath across Olivia's lips. She recalled things so sharply when she needed to. Olivia was going to lose her mind.

She distractedly, slightly too late, noticed someone walking in the hall outside, and bit back her words until a door opened, somewhere not there.

She looked down into Batch's eyes. "You're leaning toward yes?"

Batch touched Olivia's mouth, frowned at her, then said, "It doesn't make sense. You don't make any sense. Why wolves?"

It was at least not the first time she'd asked that, even if she hadn't brought it up for some time.

Olivia parted her lips for her, but Batch dragged her fingers away, to Olivia's damp hair, which she brushed back. Olivia could have curled up at her feet. Nevertheless, "I'm not only a wolf. I'm small compared to some of the others. Sometimes I worry that maybe you'll want one of them instead."

Batch tugged a piece of her hair. "I don't like you because you're tall, Olivia Hooper."

"But it helped?" Batch had said more than once that she had liked the look of Olivia first.

Batch did not answer that. She whispered, "It's nice. At night. With you. You fit around me. It's nice."

"Could be nice every night." Olivia had to make the offer.

Batch didn't answer that either, not directly. But her gaze was steady on Olivia's for a while, before she exhaled and said, "We'd have to leave them."

Now, there was a blessing. "Not Tinney," Olivia reminded her. "He comes too." Batch ducked her head, pleased, but it didn't change the look in her eyes. Olivia kissed her pretty freckled brow. "None of that, whatever you're thinking."

"You came out here by yourself." Batch was stubborn. "I've always been by myself and yet now, I can't even...."

Olivia cut her off. "Because you haven't been. Not for a while now. Your little pack—er—family have been here for you.... Well." Really, the only one in question was Ruby. And Ruby thought Olivia was charming. "We'll just have to bring them all with us," Olivia decided with a nod, petting Batch when she twitched in surprise. "I don't think they'll mind. They love you too. Anything for Primrose."

Olivia had thought Batch would like that. She hadn't expected to be kissed, hard, Batch's hands in her hair, Batch nearly pushing her to the bed before she pulled away. "Love me?" she demanded. Someone who didn't know her might have thought she was furious and not pleased and embarrassed and confused all at once.

"I told you it wasn't just the mate notion—that you're my mate." Olivia licked her lips, but sadly, it didn't draw Batch back to more kissing. So she tried explaining again. "I met you, and I liked you, and we courted, and I love you, and you are going to be my wife, and I'm going to be yours."

"But the mate—"

"You're that already." Olivia could not hear 'mate notion' one more time. "You're mine to take care of. Mate is just the foundation... the pattern, I guess, if that's easier for you. The basic idea of what you can do."

A silence followed that, but not a long one. Then Batch reached out to fiddle with one of Olivia's vest buttons. She leaned in, slow, and pressed a kiss to Olivia's throat. "Wolves," she murmured in a tone of extreme vexation. She did it again when Olivia whimpered, but it was so much more intoxicating to have Batch do this to her when Batch was done up so fine. Olivia would do anything she wanted.

"Please, Prim, honey," she begged.

Batch raised her head, startled, then studied Olivia for long enough to get an idea of what Olivia was after. She was quick that way, even if she didn't always believe what she was seeing. But she didn't come closer; she frowned. "I have to work."

"How much longer?" Olivia had no shame to waste at the moment.

"A few hours." Batch gained and lost a frown. She smiled. "You could eat while you wait. You're always hungry no matter what you say. And there's cornbread. I made it," she added, in a heartbreakingly sweet voice. "I didn't just watch this time."

That was what she'd originally said she was doing at the hotel, jobs to pay for both meals and lessons from the cook.

Batch paused. "You might also like a bath," she suggested, and paid no attention to Olivia's indignant huff. "Did you really race to get back here?"

If Batch wasn't going to pull her in for more sparking, then Olivia would pull herself in. "I was worried."

"Oh." Batch's fingers returned to Olivia's mouth, then her cheek. "I bet you are starving, then. You should go eat. Perhaps stop in to see Ruby. She has a headache. But clean up first. I'm used to seeing you pressed and bright. I almost thought you were sick, before I remembered that you said you can't be."

Olivia leaned close to take in a breath that kept her from grumbling too much. "I was courting," she reminded Batch pointedly. "I am still courting. But I rushed back just to find you looking like this and I am not allowed to touch. I am not sick but I do have a fever."

"Hogwash," Batch said faintly, after some time staring at Olivia. But then she wet her bottom lip. "I could bring you your towel?"

Olivia was burning all the way down to her toes.

"Primrose, I'll go ask for a hot bath right now."

Olivia bent down, scooping up laundry without much care and dumping it back into a smiling Batch's arms. She kissed her again while Batch was trying to steady the pile, leaving her out of breath and flushed distractingly. Then she opened the door for her.

They spilled out into the light of the hall and froze as one at the sight of Carillo in the doorway of a room a few doors down. His room, Olivia guessed, or Ruby's. He had opened the door but never closed it, and Olivia had forgotten to keep listening.

She looked away from him to Batch, who had faint marks from Olivia's hands on her red cheeks and stars in her eyes that were rapidly fading the longer she stared at Carillo.

He was too sharp a person to think this was anything other than what it was, even if he had missed the rest.

For a moment, less than a moment, there were crinkles at the corner of his eyes, there and gone. Then he nodded at each of them and slipped inside the room and firmly closed the door.

"Batch," Olivia started, ready to apologize since she hadn't been listening like she should have.

Batch blinked. "I think he was just happy not to talk about it."

Olivia stared at her, then stared some more, then decided there was more in the crinkling of that man's eyes than she would ever know. She turned away from that door, and, looking properly now, with her mind somewhat more at ease, noticed the first comb she had carved for Batch nestled among the shining waves of her hair.

Batch turned to catch her noticing. She made a face, a thoughtful, uncertain face, then, bravest creature in the world, said, "Mate," and smiled shyly before taking off down the hall.

Watching her walk away was a pleasurable sight, despite everything.

Olivia followed, as she always would, with a dazed, happy smile of her own.

The End

The Being(s) in Love Series

Magical creatures known as beings emerged from hiding amid the destruction of the First World War. Since then they've lived on the margins of the human world as misunderstood objects of fear and desire. Some are beautiful, others fearsome and powerful. Yet for all their magic and strength, they are as vulnerable as anyone when it comes to matters of the heart.

Some Kind of Magic
A Boy and His Dragon
A Beginner's Guide to Wooing Your Mate
Little Wolf
The Firebird and Other Stories
A Dandelion for Tulip
Treasure for Treasure
His Mossy Boy
Sweet Clematis
The Tales of Two Seers
Forget-Me-Not (Coming Soon)

Also By R. Cooper

Scifi and Fantasy:
Taji From Beyond the Rings
Tit for Tat
The Devotion of Delflenor
My Man Godric
The Familiar Spirits Series
A Suitable Consort (For the King and His Husband)

Contemporary:
Hottie Scotty and Mr. Porter
Play It Again, Charlie
Izzy and the Right Answer
For Better or Worse
Medium, Sweet, Extra Shot of Geek

About R. Cooper

R. Cooper lives in a pink palace by the—no. R. Cooper longs to live the life of a fictional 1980s romance novelist (but queer), but, alas, her life is actually mostly spent daydreaming and trying to write, which is at least a little Joan Wilder in spirit, including the crying over manuscripts. R. thought about gender for a while and settled on she/her/they, but don't call her a woman because it feels oogie. She likes Moonstruck maybe too much, hates fascists, does her best not to be a jerk, hides from most humans, and lives with her cat in her semi-haunted rented house somewhere between the Northern California Redwoods and wine country.
For more info, writing updates, and the occasional free story, visit www.riscooper.com

Printed in Great Britain
by Amazon